"Not hungry,"

Belvia replied. She had never been off her food until she had met Latham Tavenner.

Josy came into the sitting room with a basket arrangement of flowers.

"Why, how lovely!" Belvia said spontaneously of the splendid arrangement.

"They're from—him!" whispered Josy in scared tones.

"Him" *had* to be Latham Tavenner!

Dear Reader,

The more I thought about writing about two lovely sisters, the more I grew to like the idea. Belvia, so warm hearted and so spirited, ready to do anything for her dear—not so identical—twin. Josy, so shy, so sensitive. Both, in different ways, suffering at the hands of their devious, bullying father. Both enduring many trials and torments before they come to find true happiness.

I do so hope that after reading of Belvia and how she found that happiness you will want to read how Josy eventually came to discover true happiness, too.

Wishing you happy reading.

Yours sincerely,

Jessica Steele.

The Sister Secret
Jessica Steele

Harlequin Books

TORONTO • NEW YORK • LONDON
AMSTERDAM • PARIS • SYDNEY • HAMBURG
STOCKHOLM • ATHENS • TOKYO • MILAN
MADRID • WARSAW • BUDAPEST • AUCKLAND

ISBN 0-373-03385-0

THE SISTER SECRET

First North American Publication 1995.

Copyright © 1995 by Jessica Steele.

This edition published by arrangement with Harlequin Books S.A..

® and TM are trademarks of the publisher. Trademarks indicated with ® are registered in the United States Patent and Trademark Office, the Canadian Trade Marks Office and in other countries.

Printed in U.S.A.

CHAPTER ONE

BELVIA parked her car on the drive and let herself into her house and, dressed in old jodhpurs, she went straight to the kitchen where she was fairly certain she would find her sister busy preparing the evening meal.

'How was she?' Josy asked as soon as she saw her.

'You could come with me tomorrow and see for yourself,' Belvia suggested gently. Hetty was Josy's horse, but Josy just couldn't bring herself to go to the stables. It had not always been like that. At one time Josy had been up at the stables every minute she could spare—but that had been before Marc...

'I'm not——'

'I know, love, you're not ready yet,' Belvia interrupted quickly, her heart going out to her twin who, although like her in some ways, was so unlike her in others. 'What are we having for dinner?' Aware that Josy was hurting, she swiftly changed the conversation.

'Father's favourite.'

'Ham, peas, potatoes and parsley sauce!' Belvia recited. 'I'd better go and get showered and changed.' She was on her way out of the kitchen when she hesitated. She might have continued on her way, but saw that Josy was watching her. 'Er—do you get the feeling that Father's up to something, or is it just me and my imagination?' she asked.

'He's been a bit—um—pleasanter than usual this last couple of days, if that's anything to go by.'

'Then he *is* up to something!' Belvia needed no more confirmation than that. She knew her father of old. He could be charming—but seldom without a reason.

'He was saying last week how money was tight and how we might have to make more economies in the home.'

'According to him money's always tight,' Belvia laughed, and, unconcerned with their father's wheeling and dealing, commented, 'Thank goodness Mother left us both a little nest-egg, so we don't have to ask him for anything!'

Belvia left the kitchen and went up to her room, thinking that it was only eighteen months ago, when she and Josy had had their twenty-first birthday, that they had inherited the money left to them by their mother. It was a tidy sum, but not vast by any means. But, even so, their father had wanted them to invest the whole of it in his engineering business. Josy would have let him have the lot, but Belvia would not let her.

'He's more likely to spend it on his women than his business,' she'd persuaded her. 'And I'm sure Mummy would never have tied it up so that he couldn't get his avaricious fingers on it if she'd wanted him to have it.'

'That's a point,' Josy had agreed, remembering as Belvia did their sensitive and long-suffering mother. She'd had no money herself to start with, but the twins had been fifteen when she had inherited from a relative— and had been married for long enough to have the scales drop from her eyes. She had seen him for what he was, a philanderer and spendthrift. She had taken immediate action to ensure that, while keeping a little for herself, her two girls should have a secure future. A year later she was dead.

Belvia stripped and stepped into the shower, the water darkening her long hair. She and Josy were not identical twins: Belvia was the taller of the two and, while they both possessed dainty features, creamy complexions and the same large, deep brown eyes, Josy had hair with a reddish tint to it, while Belvia was blonde.

Belvia was the younger twin by ten minutes but, with Josy at a very early age showing signs of being painfully shy, it had seemed inborn that Belvia should protect her wherever they went.

Josy never had outgrown her shyness and, when they had left the all-girls school they attended, while Belvia had got herself a job in an office, Josy had urged her to talk to their father about letting her stay at home and keep house for them.

'Are you sure? It might be better if you got out and met a few new——'

'Oh, please, Bel!' Josy had begged in agony—and Belvia had been immediately contrite.

'All right, don't worry, I'll see to it,' she had quickly soothed.

Belvia had talked long and hard to their father, but she was sure that in the end it was purely in the interest of his own comfort that he had agreed. And matters had gone on fairly smoothly from there.

There had been a flurry of excitement when last year she and Josy had come into their inheritance. Belvia had learned to drive, purchased a good second-hand car, and had subsequently taught Josy to drive. Josy had purchased a good second-hand car too, and had then started to realise that she could also afford to buy and keep the horse she had always so passionately wanted. Belvia, her staunchest ally, had phoned around for her and found a stables which would allow her to keep a horse there.

Stepping from the shower, Belvia began towelling herself dry, a smile coming to her face as she remembered her twin's joy, how Josy had forgotten to be timid or shy the moment she had cast her eyes on Hetty.

Josy had bought Hetty without quibbling over the price, and over the next few months had spent every spare moment she could find up at the stables. Belvia had thrown up her dead-end job and, her school grades being excellent, had persuaded a firm of accountants to allow her to train with them. She had been so keen, in fact, that she would have trained without salary, but it had not come to that, and she had begun to enjoy every minute of it.

Then in the months that followed she had become aware that, while everything in her life was metaphorically coming up roses, Josy too was beginning to blossom.

She had found out why one lunch-hour when, her sister's car being in the garage for a service, she had driven up to the stables to give her a lift home, and had seen her in easy conversation with a jodhpur-clad male.

She had been more than a little amazed to see that Josy, whom she'd never heard utter more than a few words to any man near her own age, was smiling and actually *chatting*! Belvia at once felt sensitive to her sister and, while joy warmed her that Josy might be losing some of her paralysing shyness, she was on the point of going quietly away so that Josy might chat with her fellow-rider the more, when her sister turned and saw her.

'Oh, Belvia!' She welcomed her with a loving smile, and with not a stammer or a stumble in sight she introduced Marc to her.

Marc was French and, it emerged, was a groom at the stables. He was twenty-five and was, Belvia discovered, almost as shy as Josy. But he was unfailingly gentle to her sister, and Belvia could not help warming to him for that alone.

It seemed to Belvia after that that there was seldom any conversation she had with Josy in which Marc's name did not come up.

'Who's Marc?' their father, on overhearing them, enquired one day.

'He's a groom up at the stables,' Josy answered, and, to Belvia's surprise—and their father's astonishment—'May I bring him home? I'd like to intro——'

'A *groom*!' It was all Edwin Fereday said, but it was enough.

One day four months ago Josy had come and sought her out in her room and told her that she and Marc were getting married. 'Oh, darling!' Belvia had squealed on the instant, leaping up and going over to give her sister a hug.

One look at Josy's excited face, as she spoke of there being a flat available at the stables where she and Marc would live after their marriage, was all she needed to know that her sister was very happy.

'Have you decided when?' Belvia asked, her heart bursting with joy for Josy.

'Soon—next month.'

'That doesn't give us long to get ready, but we'll manage. I shall have to——' Something in Josy's suddenly haunted manner caused her to break off. 'What is it?' she asked quickly.

'I don't want a big wedding!' Josy cried in alarm.

'Nobody can make you do anything you don't want to,' Belvia soothed calmly, having had years of practice in dealing with her dear sister's sudden panics. 'I'll talk to Father if you like——' She broke off as a sudden thought struck. 'Sorry,' she smiled. 'I expect Marc will want to speak to him himself.'

'Marc would just about die at the very thought,' Josy replied, and went on to reveal that she and Marc had decided to get married in secret and go to Marc's home in France for their honeymoon, and then return to the flat.

'You're getting married without Father or me there?' Belvia queried gently. While it was unthinkable to her that her twin should marry without her there, she at the same time strove hard to remember what she had just told her—that Josy did not have to do anything she did not want to.

'Of course I want *you* there!' Josy answered at once. 'But not him. Marc's as nervous as me about it, and I'm not having Father looking down his snobby nose because Marc happens to be a groom and not a brain surgeon.'

Belvia felt more joy that the sister she had tried all her life to protect should now, in her love for the man she was to marry, be in turn protective of him.

'Are you going to tell Father before or after your wedding?' she teased, and, straightening her face, asked, 'Would you like me to tell him?'

'I'll do it—after. I'll tell him I'm going on holiday—
and I'll come and move out and tell him when I come
back.'

'Oh, love!' Belvia cried on a sudden note of anguish—
she had never thought of Josy leaving home—'I'm going
to miss you dreadfully!'

Belvia came out of her reverie on hearing the sound
of her father's car on the drive. He was home early—
perhaps he was dining out. Typically he would not have
thought to phone to let Josy know he would not be in
for dinner.

Belvia forgot about her father as she turned to go and
seek her sister out. She recalled how at Josy's wedding
she had been unable to stop crying in her joy for her—
but recalled too how, only a day later, Josy had tele-
phoned her from France, stunned and in shock that
Marc, her husband of such a short while, had been killed
in a fall while they were out riding.

Barely able to take in the tragedy that had taken place,
Belvia had sensed that her twin would not want her to
tell their father anything of what had happened, so she
had phoned his secretary and left a message that she was
going off on a week's holiday. She had gone at once to
France. She and Josy had stayed in France until after
Marc's funeral and then returned to Surrey.

There was then no question of Josy going to live in
the flat which she and Marc had got ready. And, save
for Josy saying that she did not want her father to know
she had married, that she could not bear any insensitive
remarks he might make if he knew that in the space of
just over twenty-four hours she had been married and
widowed, she had seemed to retreat into a world of her
own. So much so that Belvia, who knew her better than

anyone, began to be greatly worried when, although her sister appeared to be outwardly functioning normally, it seemed to her that she was going around in a daze. Josy still seemed to be deeply shocked when the whole of Belvia's holiday allowance from her office was used up, but she felt she could not leave Josy for hours on end by herself while she was at work.

'Aren't you going to your office today?' Josy surfaced to ask one day, seeming not to have noticed that Belvia had not been to her office for the past six weeks.

'I've given it up,' she smiled.

'But I thought...'

'I didn't think about it deeply enough before I took up the training.' Belvia made light of it. 'I've decided to take some time off while I have an in-depth think about what I want to train for.'

'Meantime you'll continue exercising Hetty for me?'

'Of course,' Belvia smiled. It was no hardship for her to go up to the stables each day, but each day she hoped that Josy would want to go and exercise her horse herself. She could not bring herself to sell Hetty on, and spoke of how much she loved her horse, but Belvia felt that only when she could go to the stables herself would she start to accept Marc's death.

Belvia left her room and went downstairs to check that Josy was all right. Marc had been dead three months now, but it still seemed like only yesterday.

'I'll make the parsley sauce if you want to go and tidy up a bit before dinner,' she offered, and Josy, with a smile of thanks, left her to it.

Contrary to Belvia's expectation, her father did not go out to dinner that night, but was seated in his usual place at the dining-room table when she helped Josy wheel the heated trolley in.

'Good day at the office?' Belvia asked, to cover for her silent sister. Only last week her father had said Josy seemed to be getting worse in that she barely spoke a word to him these days.

'As well as can be expected,' he answered pleasantly as Josy placed his soup in front of him. He's up to something, Belvia thought yet again, and wished he could give a hint so that she could prepare both of them for it.

'Business booming?' According to him, within their home four walls, it never was, so she reckoned it would keep his attention off Josy while he related how dire matters were.

'To be honest, no,' he answered right on cue. 'Though there's nothing wrong that can't be cured by a bit of financial investment.' Here it comes, Belvia thought, as she prepared to be strong for both herself and Josy. Had their mother wanted him to have their money, she would have left it to him.

'These are hard times,' she commented pleasantly as she searched for words that might be kinder than a blunt no. She was not blind to his faults and she knew he would try to bully her if she was not firm at the outset but, despite not wearing blinkers where he was concerned, he was her father and, while she might not like him very much, she loved him.

'They certainly are. Though I've every confidence that I'll weather my present little crisis.'

Not with our money you won't, Belvia thought, hoping with all she had that she could be as strong as she had to be. 'If you'd like me to go over the firm's books...'

She threw in a neat red herring, guessing, since he had not wanted her to work in the firm his grandfather had started, that he'd burn the books before he would allow her loose among the figures.

'There's no need for that,' he replied shortly, but was back to being pleasant again when, to her amazement, he leaned back in his chair and revealed, 'I've one of the keenest financiers in the country coming to dinner tomorrow evening.'

'You . . .' Belvia could not believe it. He never invited anyone home to dinner, and certainly never any keen financier! As far as she was aware, he did not know any who were *that* good. 'You've invited...' Her voice trailed off again. 'Who?' she asked.

Edwin Fereday smiled, waited a moment for effect, and then announced, 'Latham Tavenner, that's all.'

Belvia's eyes shot wide open. The name Latham Tavenner was known to her as that of one of the sharpest, if most honourable, financiers in the business. But what in creation, if her father was to be believed, was he doing having anything to do with Fereday Products? While the firm which her great-grandfather had started was quite a sizeable outfit, it would be small fry compared with the companies he had dealings with and, she would have thought, was way beneath his notice.

'What's he coming here for?' she asked suspiciously.

'Because I asked him to!' her father retorted, doing away with any pretence of pleasantness at the note of challenge in her tone.

Belvia might have inherited all her mother's sensitivity and none of her father's insensitive ways, but she had also inherited from somewhere a fair degree of intelligence. She used it then, and, knowing her father too well, she asked sharply, 'Does he know he's going to invest in Fereday Products?' and drew forth a swift and bullying reply from her parent.

'No, he doesn't!' he retorted. 'Not yet! And don't you tell him either. You just keep him——'

'*I*,' Belvia jumped in, not for a moment prepared to be bullied by him or anyone else, 'won't be here.'

'Yes, you damn well will!'

'No, I won't! Kate Mitchell, who I used to work with, is having a retirement party. I promised I'd be there.'

'Then you can just ring her up and unpromise!'

'No, I can't!'

Her father favoured her with a spleenish look, glancing from her to her sister irritatedly. And then suddenly he was smiling a smile which Belvia did not like at all, with his look coming back to her. 'Very well,' he agreed. 'If that's your last word, so be it. We'll just have to leave it to Josy to entertain our guest.'

That was when Belvia knew why she so often disliked her father. She looked from him to where Josy was just about dying a thousand deaths. She had never met Latham Tavenner either, but she did not have to: any man who was as successful and therefore as worldly as he must be would terrify her. Belvia knew in that one glance at her sister that she was crumbling just thinking about entertaining the man at their dining-table.

'So I'll stay at home!' she agreed shortly, unable to take her support from Josy now. She caught Josy's grateful look and smiled at her before she turned back to ask her father frostily, 'And what, in particular, would you like us to cook for your guest?'

'I don't give a hoot what it is, so long as you keep him sweet,' he answered.

So that was it! The something she had thought her father was up to was now very clear. He needed quite substantial investment in the firm and, the banks being unmistakably disinclined to lend him any more, he was hoping that Latham Tavenner would. Why he had invited him to dinner was a bit mystifying, but perhaps that was how these things were done—probably over a glass of port. She did not at all like her father's instruction that she 'keep him sweet', and indeed cringed at the very idea of being nice to the man purely so that her father should have him good-humoured when he asked for his money.

Belvia was up early the next morning, and was starting to feel indignant at her father's 'keep him sweet' edict. She hoped her manners were such that she would be polite and pleasant to any guest in their home.

On going downstairs, she discovered that, early as she had arisen, Josy was down before her and was already worrying about what to give their guest for dinner that night.

'What were you going to give us?' Belvia asked.

'Chicken curry, rice and a side-salad, and bread-and-butter pudding.'

'Then that's what we'll have. I'll make some celery soup, if you like.'

'Oh, would you?' Josy accepted as she attended to their father's breakfast.

He had gone to his office by eight, and at a minute past nine Josy, as if afraid Belvia might yet change her mind, was reminding her to ring Kate Mitchell to let her know that she could not come to her party.

'Hello, Kate,' Belvia greeted the kind lady who had taken her under her wing when she had first gone to train at Newman and Company. 'Enjoying your last day?'

'Mixed feelings now it's come to it,' Kate replied. 'I'll see you tonight at the party w——'

'Er—the thing is, something's cropped up...'

Five minutes later Belvia put down the phone and went in search of her sister. 'Did she mind very much?' Josy asked at once.

'A bit. I've promised I'll look in later. Much, much later,' Belvia added in a rush when she saw her twin blench. 'Father won't want either of us there when he taps Mr Tavenner for his money, so once dinner's out of the way and we've been "sweet", we'll be free to disappear.' Belvia had been about to tack on what Kate had said when she had casually asked if Newman and Company had ever had anything to do with Latham Tavenner and his outfit, but Josy was already looking uptight, and she felt it best to get away from the subject altogether.

They spent the whole of the morning giving the already spruce sitting-room and dining-room another sprucing. And what with one thing and another—all preparations made for the evening meal, right down to the best china being brought out and rinsed—it was early afternoon before Belvia felt she could leave her sister and go up to the stables to exercise Hetty.

If their father wasn't happy with their efforts that day, then hard luck, Belvia thought as she sat astride Hetty and they cantered around the countryside, though she admitted to feeling uncomfortable inside that her father was entertaining the financier purely for his own ends.

But, while not wanting to be a party to any of it, she had to own to a sneaking curiosity to see for herself the hard-headed businessman Kate had told her about. Kate had never met him, but had said he had a reputation for being a shrewd, if fair, operator. Kate had not been able to tell her much more about him other than that he was still a bachelor, though not for want of half the female population around trying to do something to alter that. Kate also thought that he and his sister, to whom he was said to be very close, had been orphaned quite young and had been brought up by relatives.

Not much to go on, Belvia mused as she returned home. If he was still a bachelor, with women running after him, then how old was he, for goodness' sake? Or was it perhaps that he was getting on in years, bald and fat, and, since it was plain that he was not short of a penny or two, was it his fortune that half the women in town were after?

She stepped lightly into the kitchen, where she found that Josy was getting into a state as the time when she was going to have to act as co-hostess came nearer.

'It'll be a breeze.' Belvia tried to bolster her up. 'Come on, leave this and go and take a shower and put something pretty on.'

Belvia went up the stairs with her and they parted to go to their separate rooms. Now what, Belvia wondered, bearing in mind that—with no time to change—she would be going on to a party later, should she wear?

'Oh, Belvia, you look stunning!' Josy exclaimed when she joined her in the kitchen. Belvia was dressed in a simple—although expensive—black dress.

'Have you taken a look at yourself?' She smiled encouragingly at Josy, who had made a tremendous effort to build her confidence and was wearing an equally simple dress of pale green that brought out the red in her hair. 'You're beautiful.'

'Tosh,' Josy responded, and Belvia went and gave her a hug.

'We're going to have to do something about your low self-esteem,' she told her seriously, then the doorbell sounded and a look of panic immediately came over her shy sister's face.

Ten minutes later Belvia judged it was time to leave the kitchen. By the time they reached the sitting-room, Josy had her panic under control. Belvia gave her a quick reassuring glance, then opened the door and led the way in—and stopped dead!

Latham Tavenner was neither bald nor fat, nor in his dotage. He had turned as they went in and, as she looked at the tall, dark-haired man in his mid-thirties, who with all-assessing, cool grey eyes looked back and appeared neither interested nor uninterested, for no known reason, her heart gave a crazy flutter.

Ridiculous. She dismissed such nonsense as not worth consideration and, knowing that Josy would stick close like glue, she went forward so that her father could make the introductions.

'This is the youngest twin, Belvia,' her father announced jovially. 'Belvia, our guest Latham Tavenner.'

'How do you do?' Belvia trotted out, extending her right hand, and felt her whole body tingle as Latham Tavenner took her hand in a firm but cursory grip then, unsmiling and without a word, dropped it and turned his attention to Josy, who was close by her side.

'And this is my other daughter, Josy.'

Protectively Belvia stood watch as Josy stretched out a nervous hand and gulped, 'Hello.'

Belvia moved a fraction closer to her and saw Latham Tavenner look from Josy to her and, after a barely perceptible pause, back to her sister again. 'Hello, Josy,' he responded, and—although Belvia had formed the view that the man did not have a smile in him—he smiled.

Although Josy's smile was a degree on the shaky side, she made it. But as Latham Tavenner let go of her hand and seemed as if he would engage her in conversation Belvia discerned in the quick look that Josy shot to her that she was signalling, 'Help me'.

'If you'll excuse us,' she butted in before he could address another word to her sister, 'Josy and I need to go and do things culinary.'

Oh, heavens, Belvia thought as she offered up a phoney smile to go with her words, and in return received the full blast of not just cool but arctic grey eyes.

Who the hell did he think he was? she fumed as she grabbed hold of Josy's arm and took her kitchenwards.

'He's terrifying!' Josy cried, the moment they were out of earshot.

'How?' Belvia queried calmly.

'Didn't you see him! Smooth, sophisticated...'

'And eats little girls for supper,' Belvia teased, on the brink of being panicky herself, she realised, for sophisticated he certainly was. And smooth. Though for herself she had no need to worry for, from what she could make of it—and it couldn't be just his suave manner or he would have smiled at her too—Latham Tavenner had taken a shine to her sister!

That notion was further endorsed when, everything ready, they moved to the dining-room and, as the meal got under way, Latham Tavenner seemed to make a point of trying to draw out her shy sister.

'Do you have a career, Josy?' he enquired pleasantly as he took a spoonful of soup.

Belvia saw her slop her own soup. 'Josy prefers to stay at home and look after Father and me,' she hurried in. Not liking him any better when he tossed her a 'who-asked-you?' look she added swiftly, 'And very well she does it, too.'

Having brought the financier's attention on herself, Belvia then had to weather his cool appraisal. Clearly he was not liking her any more than she liked him, but he brought out his 'polite guest' manners to enquire distantly, 'And do you follow a career?'

'Belvia was in training to be an accountant,' her father answered for her.

'Was?' their guest picked up.

'She got bored, and threw it up.'

Thanks, Father, Belvia fumed, and, what with one thing and another, decided she'd had enough of the pair of them.

'You manage to keep busy, no doubt?' Latham Tavenner addressed her directly.

'Some,' she managed through gritted teeth.

'What did you do today, for instance?' he wanted to know, and Belvia knew at that point that he was not one iota interested in any cooking or cleaning she might have done. All too obviously he had formed an opinion, aided by her father, that she was an idle layabout, intent on nothing but pleasure.

Far be it from her to spoil his opinion. And at least while he was talking to her he was leaving Josy alone. 'Ooh, nothing much,' she replied, sending him another

phoney smile. 'I messed about for most of the morning—
ringing up friends, that sort of thing—and then this
afternoon I went out for a ride on Hetty...'

'Hetty?'

'Josy's horse. And——'

'Doesn't Josy mind you riding her horse?'

Had they been better acquainted, she might have
kicked his shins—she'd had just about enough of him
and the way he looked down his nose at her.

'Not today,' she returned, her attempt to keep smiling
wearing thin. 'Today Josy was too busy in the house to
exercise her herself, so I thought I'd do her a favour.'

'How very generous of you!' he clipped curtly.

Good. Now perhaps he'd leave her in peace and chat
to her father! To goad her further, however, it was to
her sister that he turned, and Belvia did not know just
then whether she felt piqued or protective about that.

'Have you been riding long, Josy?' he enquired.

'Yes,' Josy whispered and, as Belvia saw the mist of
sadness that came to her sister's eyes, it was protectiveness pure and simple that rushed to the fore.

'Will you have some chutney with your curry?' she
said in a rush, picking up the mango chutney and placing
it in front of him.

'Thank you,' he accepted politely enough, but there
was a tough look in the hard grey glance he served her
with that left her with an unmistakable impression that
one Latham Tavenner had no time whatsoever for her.

Which was just fine by her—she had no time for him
either. And if he had some notion—picked up, no doubt,
from the fact that she was jobless—that she was work-
shy and that the house could be six feet deep in dust
before she would pick up a duster, it was nought to her.

Thankfully her father was taking a hand in the conversation, which was just as well. By the look of it, Latham Tavenner had given up trying to address Josy, only to be answered by Belvia. Which suited her fine, since that meant that she did not have to talk to him either.

When the meal came to an end Belvia had long since got over any feeling of awkwardness that her father was entertaining Latham Tavenner for his own ends. She was liking neither her father nor his guest just then, and in her view they deserved each other.

'That was a very nice meal,' Latham complimented her sister as he placed his napkin on the table.

'Thank you,' Josy answered quietly, but added—and Belvia wished she had not—'Belvia made the soup.'

You needn't look so surprised, she fumed crossly to herself. 'Anyone can open a tin,' she offered uncaringly, and saw a glint in his eyes that spoke of his knowing the difference between home-made and tinned—and not taking kindly to being lied to on any subject, no matter how trivial.

'If you'll excuse me.' Josy's voice penetrated, and Belvia switched her glance to where her sister was taking a tray from the room. Her duty done, she would not show her face again that night, as Belvia well knew.

And, since it was only for Josy's sake that she had delayed going to the party, Belvia could find no good reason why she should not disappear too.

'If you'll excuse me, also,' she murmured, and was on her feet when she was staggered to hear her father—in front of company—take her to task!

'Where are you off to?' he demanded.

'I'm going out,' she replied.

'At this time of night?'

Belvia stared at him, barely able to credit that, in the belief that it made him look important, he should speak to her so in front of his guest. 'I've got a date,' she replied flippantly. Casting a quick glance to Latham Tavenner, she could hardly credit either that, without bothering to hide his look of total dislike, he was staring contemptuously at her! Who *did* he think he...? He might have been orphaned at a tender age, and might well be of the opinion that she should show more respect for her father, but...

Belvia made for the door but, feeling suddenly goaded beyond what was reasonable—by the pair of them—she turned. 'After dinner is the only time he can get away from his wife,' she tossed at anyone who might be interested.

She saw her father dart a hasty glance to his guest, but cared not if she had embarrassed him. He'd asked for it—speaking to her like that in front of a guest. She slid her glance to that guest, and was shaken by the harsh anger in his face—almost malevolent! He was not embarrassed—he was furious.

Finding his look threatening, she dragged her gaze from him and, feeling oddly all of a tremble inside, she left the dining-room.

Out in the hall, away from him, she told herself not to be so ridiculous and went upstairs to collect her bag and car keys. Grief! To look like that—just because she had been saucy to her bullying father, whom she knew far better than he did!

Belvia went out to her car, but was still feeling a trifle disturbed when she arrived at Kate's party. She made herself think positively and decided that, on the up side, she had done her father a favour. Because if Latham Tavenner was so incensed about her manner to her parent, then he might feel more inclined to let him have the investment he wanted. And, on the double up side, she doubted that Latham Tavenner would accept an invitation to dine at her home a second time. Which meant, happily, that she would never have to see him again.

CHAPTER TWO

FOR all that the party was good, Belvia came home dogged, as she had been at the party, by thoughts of Latham Tavenner. Damn the man, she fumed, then showered and climbed into bed, to sleep badly and dream of the wretched man.

She slept late and found that her father, off on his weekend pursuits, had already left the house to pick up his present lady-love.

'Good party?' Josy asked, looking up from stacking the dishwasher as Belvia walked into the kitchen.

'It was, actually,' she replied, and sank down on a kitchen chair and related some of the highlights.

'Coffee?' Josy enquired.

'Gasping!'

Josy busied herself making them both a cup of coffee, and then, placing a beaker down in front of Belvia, commented, 'You were shouting in your sleep last night.'

'Was I?' Belvia enquired, startled. In childhood she had shouted out in her sleep whenever she was disturbed about something, and she had gone through another bout of it shortly after her mother had died. 'I haven't done that in years. Was I yelling anything interesting?'

Josy smiled. 'Just gibberish.' And, her smile fading, 'Anything worrying you, Bel?'

'Not a sausage,' Belvia laughed, 'save for the mountain of clearing-up we left in the dining-room.'

'I'd have done it last night, only——'

26

'I know,' Belvia cut in gently, fully aware that, but for the fact that Josy had risked bumping into Latham Tavenner around the sitting-room area, she would have set to in the dining-room after the man had left it. Apparently there was something about the cool, detached man that disturbed both of them. She had been thinking of him when she had gone to bed last night, and could think of no other reason why she should have been visited by a return of shouting out in her sleep.

What she needed was exercise, and plenty of it, she decided, and quickly downed her coffee. 'I'll go and investigate the dining-room,' she remarked, getting to her feet.

'Don't you want any breakfast?'

'Not hungry,' Belvia replied, and, at the ridiculous thought that she had never been off her food until she had met Latham Tavenner, she realised that she was giving a man in whose company she had spent not much more than an hour far too much time.

She was in the sitting-room later that morning, plumping up cushions, when Josy went by to answer a ring at the door. She heard the door open and then close, and stopped what she was doing altogether when, her face pale, her eyes worried, Josy came into the sitting-room with a basket arrangement of flowers.

'Why, how lovely!' Belvia said spontaneously of the splendid arrangement.

'They're from—him!' Josy whispered in scared tones.

'Him' *had* to be Latham Tavenner! 'Well, it's only a thank-you for his dinner last night,' Belvia replied bracingly.

'But *your* name isn't on the card!'

Belvia would have been astonished if it had been. 'So?' she enquired.

'You helped cook dinner too. I—think he likes me,' Josy said worriedly.

It's for certain he doesn't like me, Belvia thought, and could not make up her mind whether she appreciated his honesty in leaving her off the card, or if she thought him oafish and sadly lacking in the manners department for the omission.

'Who could help liking you?' she teased—to no avail.

'Will you put them in your room?' Josy begged, clearly not wanting to catch a glimpse of them anywhere and so be reminded of the man whose sophistication all too obviously awed her.

'Of course,' Belvia replied easily before she could think—and then realised that she did not want to be reminded of the beastly man either. 'Or, better still, I'll take them to Tracey when I go to the stables this afternoon. She'll enjoy them, I'm sure.'

'Oh, she will,' Josy replied, starting to look easier. Tracey was one of the grooms up at the stables and had a positive passion for flowers. 'Only don't tell her that they came for me, will you?'

'I'll say they came from one of my many admirers,' Belvia laughed, liking the humour of that thought—an admirer of hers was something which Latham Tavenner most definitely was not.

The rest of the weekend passed without incident and Belvia was pleased to see that by Sunday evening, given that Josy was still suffering over the loss of her husband, as she would be for some time to come, she was otherwise back on a more even keel and calmer over Latham Tavenner's attentions to her.

Belvia got out of bed on Monday morning and felt more on an even keel herself. She went downstairs, saw her father in conversation with her sister through the open breakfast-room door, popped her head in and offered a 'Good morning,' then took herself off to the kitchen. She had just put a couple of slices of bread in the toaster when Josy joined her. 'I've put the toast in for us,' she began, but stopped when she saw that Josy was looking agitated. 'What's up, Jo?' she asked.

'I've just had a lecture from Father on the subject of shaping up and being more amenable to guests he brings into this house!'

By 'guests', since he seldom invited anyone home, Belvia knew her father could only mean Latham Tavenner. And that angered her. But while on the one hand she wanted to go straight away to see their father and let him know that she and her sister had not the smallest desire to be included in his devious games to finance Fereday Products, she felt it was more important just then to try to calm Josy down.

'Well, don't let it throw you, love. Since Father only invites a guest home once in a flood, you haven't a thing to worry about.'

'But what if he does?'

'He won't,' Belvia replied firmly, though she could see that Josy was far from convinced. 'And if he does, then you can make yourself scarce, and I'll look after Mr Latham Tavenner personally,' she promised lightly.

Josy still did not look reassured, and the day got under way badly, with their father going off to his office and with Belvia giving serious thought to her and her sister finding somewhere to live on their own and moving out. The only trouble with that, she mused as she took ad-

vantage of a lovely summer day and went into the garden
to do some weeding, was that Josy was so shy with
strangers, and any move they made would have to in-
volve meeting new people.

She still had Josy on her mind when half an hour later
she went indoors for a cold drink. Would it be better
for her sister to be made to meet new people? she wondered, but at once cancelled that idea. Seldom a day
went by now that she did not find her twin staring into
space, hurting and still distraught over losing Marc. How
could she think of...?

Belvia's thoughts came to an abrupt end when Josy
came into the kitchen, looking more upset than ever.

'What's the matter?' she asked urgently.

'He's just rung!'

'Who?' Belvia asked, leading her over to a chair.

'Latham T-Tavenner!' Josy answered distractedly.

Belvia's breath caught; she had not anticipated this.
Without haste she pulled up a kitchen chair close to her
sister. 'What did he want?' she enquired as calmly as
she could.

'There's a charity concert thing on in London tonight—some big affair. He's got tickets and wondered
if I'd like to go.'

'You said no?'

'How *could* I?' Josy cried. 'Not after Father lecturing
me this morning. He'd go wild if I had to tell him I
turned down a date with the man he's breaking his neck
to get in with.'

'All right, all right, keep calm,' Belvia instructed,
seeing she was close to going to pieces. 'So what did
you tell him?'

Josy took a shaky breath as she strove hard to recapture her self-control. 'At first, when I knew who it was, I just couldn't say a word. Then, quite pleasantly, he said, "You haven't forgotten me already, I hope," and I panicked a bit and—probably after what you said about you personally looking after him—I asked him if he wanted to speak to you.'

I'll bet that thrilled him, Belvia thought, but could see that Josy was in no mind to appreciate the humour of her thoughts. 'So he politely told you no, and then asked you out. And, since you didn't say no, you must have said yes,' she prompted.

'I must have done—he's sending a car for me this evening,' Josy gulped. 'Oh, Bel, I can't go! He's so sure of himself, while I'm so unsure of just about absolutely everything—he positively terrifies me!'

Belvia spent the next five minutes promising that her uncertainty about everything would pass, and that—while admittedly Josy had always been desperately shy—it must all be part and parcel of the dreadful loss she had suffered. 'And,' she ended, 'if you're so terrified of the man, then I wouldn't dream of letting you go anywhere with him.'

'You wouldn't?'

Belvia shook her head.

'But—what about Father? I can't let him down!'

'Leave Father to me—I'll ring him at his office.'

Belvia got on the phone straight away. Her father was not in his office and her call was diverted to Vanessa Stanley, his secretary of the last five years; according to him, the fluffily pretty woman was as hard inside as she appeared soft outside. Though whether this was because he had chanced his arm with her, only to be told she preferred men nearer her own age—the late twenties, Belvia could only conjecture.

'If you'd like to hold, I can go and find him,' Vanessa offered. 'Or shall I ask him to ring you?'

'I'll wait, shall I?' The sooner she got something sorted out for Josy the better.

The line went dead, and then, what seemed like an age later, her father, not taking kindly to being phoned at the office, was grumpily enquiring, 'I hope the house isn't on fire?'

'Latham Tavenner has phoned asking Josy out to-night, and she can't go!' Belvia told him bluntly, her spirits dropping—from the sound of it, she had caught him at a bad time.

'Why can't she go?' he wanted to know, equally bluntly.

'Because he terrifies her, that's why!' she answered aggressively.

'Rubbish!'

'Well, she's not going.'

'Put her on the line.'

Over her dead body. 'She's upstairs,' Belvia lied.

'Then you just tell her from me that we need his money. For God's sake, all she's got to do is go out with him—he won't eat her.'

'But she's shy! You know she is. She'll——'

'Then it's about time she grew out of it! Tell her from me that she's to go and that's an end to it!' With that, in a fine rage, her father slammed down the phone.

Stars above, how her mother had put up with him all those years...!

'What did he say?' Belvia was so angry that she had forgotten for a moment that Josy was in the same room.

'I—er—caught him at the wrong moment,' she had to confess, and thought fleetingly of suggesting again that she and Josy moved out. Then she saw that Josy looked near to tears, and it just wasn't fair—the little love hadn't been widowed four months! It just wasn't right that she should be put through this! 'You're not going,' she stated unequivocally. 'I'd sooner go myself.' It would not come to that, of course. 'Would you pass me the phone book?'

'What are you going to do?'

'You're going to have a migraine.'

Josy looked hopeful. Ten minutes later and she was looking downcast again. Belvia had got through to the Latham Tavenner building, and had even got through to his PA, but when she asked to speak to him, she had been politely, pleasantly, but firmly blocked.

'May I take a message for you?'

'I particularly wanted to speak to him personally.'

'Who did you say was calling?'

She hadn't said. 'My name is Fereday, Belvia Fereday,' she replied, and that was when the PA had said Mr Tavenner was out of town all day—and Belvia did not believe it for a minute. Though since it was highly unlikely that he had told his PA he had dined in her company on Friday and had taken an instant dislike to her, she did not know quite why she did not believe that Latham Tavenner was out of town—she just didn't. 'Should I leave a message, will he get it today?' she asked—her last hope.

'I'm afraid I can't promise that. Mr Tavenner sometimes rings through at the end of the day, but it's by no means certain.'

Belvia toyed with the idea of leaving a message that his date for that evening was off. But Josy would want her to give an excuse—and what excuse was there? On thinking about it, any migraine she invented could be better by this evening and, by speaking to Josy personally only a short while ago, he knew that she was not in bed with flu.

'I'll leave it, thank you,' she said politely, added, 'Goodbye' and hung up. 'Look.' She addressed her twin seriously as she turned round to see that Josy had already realised the negative result of that phone call. 'You don't *have* to go!'

A shuddering kind of sigh escaped Josy. 'I do,' she answered. 'For Father's sake, I have to.'

'Oh, damn,' Belvia groaned, and knew that, love him or hate him, when it came to the crunch, neither of them could let their father down. She let go a shaky breath too, loathing the whole of this as much as her sister did. Though when a glance at her showed that Josy seemed to be wilting where she sat, Belvia started to grow angry. This just was not on! 'You're not going!' she stated. No argument.

'I have to.'

'No, you don't. You——'

'Let's face it Bel,' Josy interrupted, 'we can't get in touch with him, and he's sending a car for me. By the time the chauffeur turns up without me, it will be too late for him to rustle up another female—date. That,' she ended in a choked voice, 'is certain to make it a foregone conclusion that he'll want nothing to do with any of the Fereday family again. I have to k-keep my word—the Fereday word.'

In the world of high finance a person's word meant everything; Belvia knew that. Oh, stuff it, she fumed, and knew then that if the Fereday word was to be kept one of them had to go. It was with a great deal of reluctance that she realised it was time to put her money where her mouth was. Though Latham Tavenner was not going to like it any more than she was.

'So,' she smiled, 'what am I going to wear?'

The only thing Belvia was grateful for when, right on time that evening, a sleek limousine pulled up outside was that, as sometimes happened, her father was not yet home. It was taking all she had to go through with this— she could do without his objections and arguments.

'Oh, Belvia, you look lovely!' Josy exclaimed as she went with her to the door, admiring the look of her in her strapless sheath of white satin, her only jewellery a pair of pendant crystal ear-rings.

Belvia needed to hear that. She was not shy nor timid where men were concerned, unlike her sister, but her insides were quaking. Lord above only knew how Josy would have been feeling had she been the one dressed in all her finery on her way out.

That thought alone was sufficient for her to know she was doing the only thing possible. Josy could just not have coped. 'Now, remember.' She went through what they had decided to tell their father again. 'If Father cuts up rough when he gets in, tell him you've got a tummy upset and that rather than have you throw up in the car, and in particular rather than break the Fereday word, I've gone in your stead.'

Josy nodded solemnly, and Belvia, her long blonde hair swept upwards in an elegant style on top of her head, went out to where the chauffeur immediately sprang to open the rear door of the most splendid limousine. Belvia got in and, with a cheery wave to Josy hovering on the doorstep, they were away.

What Latham Tavenner was going to say when he saw her she did not dare think, and by the time they were approaching the theatre, Belvia's insides were churning so much that she felt the tummy upset Josy was to tell their father she was suffering with was about to be visited on her.

There was no sign of Latham Tavenner when the limousine drew to a stop. The chauffeur got out and, with her insides in more of a knot than ever, Belvia prepared to get out too. Then the passenger door was opened—and suddenly it was not the chauffeur who stood there but, having appeared from nowhere, Latham Tavenner!

Oh, heavens! He looked magnificent in evening clothes! But as he stood there and just stared at her, he was clearly quite unable to believe his eyes. Belvia opened her mouth, her rehearsed excuses at the ready, but, with her stomach churning and her heart banging away against her ribs, all at once she could not remember a word of them.

Which left her to do the only thing possible. She dipped her head to avoid looking at him, and stepped elegantly out of the streamlined vehicle.

The next second she was standing close up to the athletically built financier—and would not have been at all surprised had he pushed her back into the limousine and instructed the chauffeur to deliver her back whence she came. For it was all there as he recovered from seeing that the wrong Fereday twin had turned up and snarled, 'I invited your sister, not you!'

His tone was what she needed—it nettled her. 'We——' she began snappily—and that was as far as she got. For abruptly, not giving her chance to say another word, Latham Tavenner caught hold of her by her upper arm. Though not, she swiftly realised, to push her back in the vehicle, but to turn her in the direction which they were to go.

'We're holding everything up!' he grunted, and, plainly irritated to find himself lumbered with her for the evening, he bent and closed the passenger door, and as the vehicle slid away and another pulled up in its place Belvia saw that cars were queuing up to drop off their passengers. The next she knew was that the firm hand was on her upper arm again and, while flash cameras seemed to be going off everywhere, Latham Tavenner was instructing her tersely—through a seemingly smiling mouth—to 'Try and look as though you're enjoying yourself—you'll probably see the result in the paper tomorrow.'

Belvia smiled and hated him, and walked with him into the theatre and into the crowded foyer, and was glad with all her heart that it was she who was there and not her twin. Aside from having this brute of a man steering her around, Josy would never have been able to cope with the attention of the Press and television cameras, even if well aware that it was more her escort they would be interested in than her. Nor, as Latham was halted here and there by people he knew and exchanged a few words, and occasionally introduced her to someone, could Josy have coped with that either.

To Belvia's surprise, however, while she knew without doubt that her escort must be furious to find himself having to put up with her, he was unfailingly polite to her in front of other people. Though she guessed it was only a matter of time before she felt the whiplash edge of his tongue.

They had made it to their seats, with about five minutes to go before the performance was about to start, when Belvia gave up all pretence of appearing intent on the programme he had purchased for her—and decided to get in first. Impulsively she turned to look at him. Though when he, sensing her movement, turned to look at her too and stared arrogantly down at her the words died in her throat.

But it was important for her father that she get through to him, so, 'I apologise that I'm here and not Josy...' she managed—ye gods, arrogant did not begin to cover it as one superior eyebrow went aloft! 'But when Josy was taken suddenly ill...' She ploughed doggedly on.

'Your sister is ill?'

'A twenty-four hour bug,' she lied brazenly. 'It was important, we both felt, that the word of a Fereday should be kept. So...' She let the fact that she was there finish the sentence for her, and was just congratulating herself that she had assured him that he could rely on a Fereday when she saw his arrogant look change to one of amazement.

'You thought I'd be inconsolable if the car arrived empty?' he queried incredulously.

'No, of course not. But——'

'Oh, shut up,' he grated, and for the first time in her life she came within an ace of punching a man on the nose.

'Bastard!' she muttered, and the lights in the theatre went down—and she would have sworn she heard his smothered laugh! Actually heard him laugh! As if he had heard her muttered expletive—as if she had amused him!

Belvia, while looking at the stage, saw and heard nothing of the first half-hour of the concert. Good grief, what was happening to her? She had never called anyone a bastard in her life! And what was more, if asked, she would have said she never would. The word was just not part of her vocabulary—or so she would have said.

It was him, his fault! He had goaded her to it. Well, she would be hanged if she would apologise. Come to think of it, she had never thought she would want to set about anyone physically either. But that too was his fault! Who the devil did he think he was, telling her to shut up? Infuriating swine!

By the time the interval arrived, Belvia had cooled down sufficiently to realise that, although it would irk her beyond measure, for her father's sake she was going to have to make amends for that 'bastard'.

She hoped, in a way, that she *had* amused Latham Tavenner, come to think of it. Because, if he was in a good humour, she might be able to get in a tactful word with which to ask him to leave Josy alone.

That chance, however, did not come. 'Would you care for a drink?' her escort enquired when the lights went up.

She much preferred to sit where they were so that she could talk to him—tactfully. 'No, thanks,' she smiled, realising as she stared into his strong, good-looking face that she must have been mistaken about having amused him, because his expression was now as arrogant—not to mention hostile—as she remembered it.

'You won't mind if I do, I'm sure,' he commented suavely, and so much for her decision to stay and talk

because—and she was having a hard time taking it in—
he did no more than get up and leave her!

The pig, the utter pig! She hoped the bar was dry by
the time he got there. She was still fuming many minutes
later when, startling her out of her thoughts, a man
somewhere around her own age came and sat down in
the empty seat next to her.

'Didn't I see you with Latham Tavenner?' he asked,
turning sideways in the seat Latham had vacated.

'Er—yes,' she agreed.

'Rodney Phillips,' the man introduced himself. 'At a
rough guess I'd say I've not much time before he comes
back—I don't suppose you'd like to let me have your
phone number, would you?'

After so much tension, it was a great relief to find she
felt like laughing. Rodney Phillips was transparent, and
harmless. 'Not a chance,' she laughed.

'Oh, you're so beautiful!' he exclaimed, and then, as
if fearing he was being too familiar, 'Can I get you an
ice-cream or something?' he asked earnestly.

'What you can do, Phillips, is get out of my seat,'
Latham Tavenner addressed to his earnest back.

Like someone shot, Rodney Phillips sprang to his feet.
'Sorry, sir,' he apologised, and as unexpectedly as he
had arrived so he went.

'Does he work for you?' Belvia enquired.

He nodded, and took his seat. 'Was he annoying you?'
he enquired crisply.

'I enjoyed talking to him,' she replied—and take that
whichever way you care to, she added inwardly.

Aggravatingly, Latham Tavenner did not take it that
she was hinting that it was nice to have somebody around
to be able to talk to, but made it sound as though she

liked to make a conquest of every male she came into contact with by commenting grimly, 'He's too young for you!' Again Belvia wanted to thump him. Was he warning her to keep away from his staff?

Belvia sat and fumed for the rest of the performance and, for herself, would have walked back to Surrey rather than spend another moment more in his company than she had to when the concert was over. But there was her father, who was relying on Latham Tavenner investing his money in his company, and, more importantly to her, there was Josy.

'Thank you. It was very good, wasn't it?' She forced the words out between her teeth as they made their way out from the theatre.

'I expect you're hungry,' he offered, which in her view was no sort of a reply, but it did hold a hint that he might feed her. Surely then she could get a word in to ask him to leave her sister alone, although, for her father's sake, it would have to be done with the utmost tact.

'Starving,' she lied; she had been too stewed up to eat a crumb before she had left home, and felt pretty much the same now.

As if by magic, the chauffeur-driven car she had arrived in pulled up alongside as they walked to the edge of the pavement. Latham said not a word to her as they drove, but she was unworried by that. She had better things to do—such as sorting her words into some kind of order.

They arrived at an old, stately-looking building and, getting out, Belvia realised he had brought her to his club to eat. Good, she thought as they went in and she

looked about. She would have a far better chance to talk
to him in these discreet confines than in any nightclub.

'I tried to phone you,' she opened, with the latest of
her rehearsed lines, 'but——'

'Why the hell would you want to do that?' he demanded, and Belvia did not need any more than that to
have it confirmed he did not like her and would take the
gravest exception to her taking advantage of the fact that
he had dined in her home last Friday.

'Surprising as it may seem—I don't fancy you!' she
hissed, and was saved from ruining everything and
upending the water-jug over his head when the waiter
arrived with their first course. It gave her the chance to
get herself under control. So she bit down the words to
tell Latham Tavenner to go and take a running jump,
and dipped her spoon into her soup.

'Mmm, this is good,' she remarked civilly, much too
preoccupied to have any idea what it tasted like. 'Er—
I'm sorry Josy couldn't make it this——'

'Your date for this evening obviously couldn't make
it either!' he cut in sharply.

'My d——?' What *was* it about this man? 'Men aren't
in the habit of breaking dates with me!' she erupted, her
chin tilting at a lofty angle. She did not like the hard
glint that came to his eyes, and knew that she would
have been better staying quiet.

'My God, you need taking down a peg or two!' he
rapped.

She hoped he did not think he was the man to do it!
Not that she agreed with him, anyway. Though as it belatedly dawned on her that she was a mile away from
being as tactful as she had decided she must be, she

fought hard to hide the antagonism which this man aroused in her.

'Look, I'm sorry if I've offended you,' she began placatingly, and saw from his distrustful look that he was not placing any faith in her apology. 'But the reason I tried to phone you was because Josy had a sudden tummy upset...' She took a glance at him from beneath her lashes—and saw he was not believing that either. 'And I thought—if I *could* get in touch with you—that I could explain about Josy not—um—being well.'

'And when you couldn't get in touch with me—you decided to come in her place?'

The way he put it made it sound as if he thought she was some egotist to believe for a moment that he would consider herself a good substitute for Josy.

Oh, to blazes with him, Belvia fumed as her anger against him once more spiralled. Suddenly she checked. Anger was just something she could not afford right now. She had to think only of her sister, and forget all about her own emotions.

She looked across at him and knew that, even without his abrasive manner, her gentle, saintly sister would go under if she had to go out with him. He was so virile, so, so—absolutely everything. Poor, sad Josy just *had* to be protected.

'Um—if——'

'You seem to be struggling?' he interrupted urbanely. 'Surely not?'

Viper! She smiled. 'I'm searching for tact,' she confessed.

'Which means, no matter how you dress it up, that I'm not going to like it.'

Shrewd was not in it. 'Well, the thing is, Josy, my twin . . .'

'I know who she is.'

Somehow Belvia managed to keep the smile on her face, even while endearing thoughts of burying an axe in his head intruded. 'The thing is,' she forced herself to go on, 'Josy is very shy. Extremely shy,' she added for good measure.

'She sounded all right on the phone this morning.'

'She's also extremely well-mannered,' Belvia stated crisply, and had to weather his look that asked if they had both been brought up by the same parents.

'You're trying to tell me something?' he enquired mockingly.

Her temper flared; she forced it down, though her tone was sharper than she had meant when she told him, 'My sister is not used to men!'

'But you undoubtedly are!' he rapped.

Damn him, one of these days . . .

Her temper cooled. She doubted that she would ever get the chance to land him one—as he so richly deserved.

'Actually, I'm not,' she replied, and felt her palms itch to come into sharp contact with his face at the look of total derision which he did nothing to hide. 'But . . .' She dug her heels in—she'd finish this if it killed her. 'This isn't about me, it's about Josy and the fact that . . . Well, just this evening for a start—all those people, the cameras, the TV people—she's not used to that sort of thing, she'd . . .'

'She'd never cope?' he suggested.

'She wouldn't.'

'But you're not used to it either—and you coped.' Her beautiful brown eyes shot wide—she had not thought he had noticed. Not that he was offering a compliment of any kind.

'I'm not Josy,' she said quietly. 'I'm different.'

'I'll agree there—I've never seen such a pair of mismatched twins.'

'Don't dress it up—insult me!' she snapped—and actually saw his mouth twitch. A moment later and she knew from his stern expression that he was not in the slightest amused by her sharp tongue. And, oh, Lord, she realised, she was going to have to stop firing up like this! But his intimation that Josy was so likeable while she was quite the opposite had been hurtful—though why it should be hurtful when she couldn't stand him either was a mystery. She took a deep and steadying breath. Tact, she realised, was wasted here, so as calmly as she could, her voice taut from the control she was exercising, she stated distinctly, 'What I'm asking, Mr Tavenner, is that, if you feel you have to get in touch with my sister again, you bear in mind her painful shyness, and treat her with every kindness.'

Latham Tavenner surveyed her coolly, his grey eyes unhurriedly taking in her clear, creamy skin, her delicate features. His glance strayed to her mouth and lingered there, before going up to her eyes again. He drawled, insolently almost, 'I treat all women as they deserve.'

Belvia could hardly believe her ears. In the next split second, however, as what he was really saying hit home—that she deserved to be treated no better than he was treating her—she was instantly outraged! In that moment she knew that she hated him more than she had hated anybody in the whole of her life!

'Thanks!' she spat—and stood up. He was on his feet too. She ignored him—and other interested diners—and, with her head in the air, she sailed furiously out of the dining-room.

CHAPTER THREE

BELVIA awoke on Tuesday morning, opened her eyes, and groaned. Oh, grief—too late now to regret her hasty temper. It was done.

She was in the middle of contemplating how, so far as she could remember, she had never had much of a temper, still less such a hasty one—so it had to be all *his* fault that he could provoke her to such anger—when her bedroom door opened and Josy came in with a cup of tea for her.

'It's late?' Belvia guessed.

'You were late in. Father's just gone to his office, but I couldn't wait any longer to hear if everything was all right last night. Did...?'

'You told Father I'd gone to keep the appointment?' Belvia asked, sitting up and playing for time as she tried to sort out in her head just how much she should tell her twin.

'I told him,' Josy confirmed. 'And save for grunting something cutting to the effect that at least one of his daughters was blessed with a sense of duty, he just had his dinner and went out.'

'Not to worry,' Belvia smiled. 'I don't think Latham Tavenner was too delighted that it was me in place of you last night, but his manners, in front of other people, were impeccable,' she stated honestly, deciding at that moment to keep quiet about her own abominable manners in walking out on Latham mid-way through

47

their soup course—she was feeling a tiny bit guilty that morning.

'He—didn't cut up too rough?'

'I explained you had a tummy upset, and he must have swallowed it,' she went on, wondering when she had become such an accomplished liar, 'because after the show he took me to his club for dinner.'

'Oh!' Josy exclaimed, and her feeling of relief was obvious in her face. 'Do you think he might transfer his attention on to you now?' she asked hopefully.

Belvia knew full well that there was not the smallest chance of that. 'You never know,' she smiled and, hoping to avoid further questioning, added, 'Thanks for the tea—I'd better get up.'

Belvia was barely out of bed when thoughts of Latham Tavenner pushed through her firm efforts to keep him out of her head. She had only been in his company twice but she found his good looks, his manliness unforgettable. She had been ill-mannered to get up and leave him the way she had—she could admit that this morning. But he had been very much out of order in her opinion, not even to pretend to believe her lies about Josy being ill, to tell her to shut up the way he had, to leave her sitting there in the theatre while he went and had a drink, and then insolently to tell her that he was treating her as he believed she deserved—and then expect her to sit there and eat with him!

She had a quick shower, realising she was angry again, and got dressed not caring a damn that she had walked out on him—she would do it again any time. She doubted, though, that she'd be so lucky a second time as to espy the chauffeur of the limousine in conversation with one of the club staff.

'You're ready to go home, Miss Fereday?' he had enquired courteously on seeing her alone and heading for the outside doors—by the sound of it he had been instructed to wait around to deliver her back to Surrey.

'Mr Tavenner will not need you again this evening,' she had been still angry enough to tell him, albeit with a smile. 'Shall we go?'

She was still not regretting any of her actions when she went down the stairs to join her sister. But as the day wore on she began to be visited, with a growing frequency, by thoughts about what her actions might have done to her father's chances of doing business with Latham Tavenner's company.

She took herself off to exercise Hetty and returned to her home just after three, to be passing the phone in the hall when it rang. She picked it up, and heard the cool, detached tones of the man who had been in her head for most of that day.

'You made it back to darkest Surrey, then?' he enquired arrogantly.

Since it had taken until now for him to pick up a phone to enquire, she doubted that her safe arrival home was on his list of priorities. But she swallowed the ire which just hearing him, arrogant and cool, produced.

He had not said who he was, and neither had he asked which twin she was. 'Thank you, yes.' She hauled her manners back into shape. 'How are things in darkest London?' she returned, well aware that he had not dialled her number merely to dally with her over the phone but realising that, for her father's sake, she had better make some effort.

Latham Tavenner, she was swiftly to realise, had no thought of doing the same, for, ignoring her question, he asked, 'Is Josy there?'

'What do you want her for?' she asked snappily, her protective claws unsheathed on the instant.

The taut silence at the other end spoke volumes, and that was before, his tone stiff with annoyance at her impudence, he spelt it out. 'I don't think that has anything to do with you.'

'It has *everything* to do with me!' Belvia countered. 'I told you last night how very shy she is!'

'Do you vet all her personal phone calls like this?' he barked.

'Why wouldn't I?' she erupted, that word 'personal' somehow catching her on the raw. Crazily, she did not like the thought of him getting 'personal' with her sister—and for one horrifying moment had the oddest sensation that that did not stem from any sense of protectiveness over Josy. Abruptly Belvia sent that peculiar notion on its way but, because of it, felt sufficiently weakened to be placatory once more as she lied, 'Josy's—er—still not well.'

'Oh, what a pity. She's so sweet and charming.' Belvia could almost hear him thinking 'unlike you'. 'I was hoping she might be up to coming out somewhere with me this evening.'

At that very moment Josy came quietly down the stairs and into the hall. 'I don't think she is but, if you'll hold on, I'll go and ask her.' With that she put her hand over the mouthpiece. 'Latham Tavenner,' she said in an undertone to her twin. 'He wants to know how you are today and if you'd like to go out somewhere.'

Josy was starting to look alarmed before she had half finished. 'No!' she exclaimed, vigorously shaking her head, distinctly starting to panic that he had not, as she had hoped, transferred his attentions to her sister.

'It's all right, don't worry,' Belvia assured her quickly, and, taking her hand from the mouthpiece, 'I'm sorry, Latham,' she told him, ploughing on even while she felt aghast at the natural way his name had just seemed to fall from her lips, 'but Josy feels she wouldn't be very good company just now.'

'Another time perhaps. I'll phone again,' he threatened as he ended his call.

Belvia put the phone down, knowing that she just could not tell Josy that last bit—she would be on thorns waiting for the phone to ring.

'What did he say?' she asked agitatedly.

Belvia smiled reassuringly. 'That he hopes you'll soon be better.'

Some lies, Belvia mused, as later that day she helped Josy with the evening meal, are essential. Already her sister seemed to have put the memory of that phone call behind her, and was even starting to look a shade less hunted. Was this the beginning of Josy starting to come to terms with Marc's death? She did hope so—the poor love had suffered enough.

Josy's sufferings were far from over, Belvia discovered when, with their father home early, the three of them sat down to dinner. For he was at pains to tell them how desperate matters were at Fereday Products and how, with his renewed entreaty to the banks for more capital falling on stony ground, it was now more essential than ever that Latham Tavenner looked on him favourably.

A squeak of an 'Oh!' escaped Josy's lips, and drew Edwin Fereday's attention.

'What was that "Oh" about?' he wanted to know.

'He—Latham Tavenner—he rang today,' Josy revealed shakily.

'Mmm—interesting,' her father replied, a speculative light appearing in his eyes which Belvia did not miss. 'What did he ring about?'

'I didn't speak...'

'I took the call,' Belvia took over.

'So what did he want?'

Her father was sounding tough, but that was when Belvia found that she had the ability to lie her head off without blushing, if it was to shield her sister. To lie to her father to shield herself, she could not. 'He wanted to speak to Josy—only I wouldn't let him,' she owned up—and brought his wrath down upon her head.

'You wouldn't *let* him?' he raged. 'Have you any idea what you're messing with here—the jobs that will go to the wall if I have to close down? How dare you offend the one person who can get us out of the hole we're in?'

'He wasn't offended!' she defended. 'Well, a little bit annoyed, perhaps,' she had to concede. 'But——'

'But nothing. It doesn't matter a damn to you, does it, that I might go out of business? That——'

'Of course it matters.'

'It sounds like it. Just because you have money of your own, everyone else can——'

'You can have my money if you want it,' Belvia cut in rashly before she could think.

'And mine,' Josy rushed in.

Their offer stopped him dead in his tracks. But, inside a very few seconds, he was off again. 'It's too late for that now. I need more than the pair of you have put together. I could have had it too, if only you'd been more pleasant to Latham Tavenner. It's just too bad of you, Belvia.'

Belvia did not like his laying all the blame at her door, though she started to realise that there was no one else whom he could, or perhaps should, blame, 'I'm sorry,' she apologised—and brought more of his spleenishness down about her.

'Sorry's an empty word unless you intend to right the wrong,' he told her heavily.

'Right the wrong?' she queried. 'How can I do that? Latham Tavenner wants to date Josy, not me!' She glanced at her twin, saw she was starting to look anxious again, and turned back to her father. 'I don't think Josy should have anything to do with him if she doesn't w——'

'You're the one who messed things up! It wouldn't hurt you to keep him sweet by ringing him and inviting him to dinner tomorrow.'

Like blazes she would! Belvia had already mentally rejected his suggestion out of hand—and then she saw her father watching her as if to say, See how empty your 'sorry' is when put to the test. She remembered too how he had spoken of jobs going to the wall, his staff losing their jobs, their livelihoods, and if all she had to do to get him the investment he needed—for himself and his workers—was to invite Latham Tavenner to dinner tomorrow evening, then was it such a high price to pay?

'He won't come for me.' Some stray strand of fear still held her back—though she was uncertain just then whether that fear was for Josy or for herself.

'Then tell him it's your sister's wish that he join us for dinner.' Her father at once knocked that argument away.

'I've already told him Josy isn't well. She won't be well enough by tomorrow to cook him dinner,' Belvia still prevaricated, and received one of her father's bad-tempered looks for her trouble.

'Well, for goodness' sake invite him for some time this week!' he bawled.

Belvia refused to be cowed. 'I don't know his home phone number.'

'I'll give it to you,' he replied, and took out his pen and a piece of paper from his diary, wrote the number down—then in angry silence finished his meal, and went out for the evening.

It was time, Belvia well knew, for her again to put her money where her mouth was. 'Is it all right with you if I ring Latham Tavenner?' she asked Josy.

'I don't see that you've got very much choice,' Josy replied bravely, and Belvia wondered if she would be putting too much pressure on her just now if she suggested that she would like her to think very seriously about the two of them leaving home in the near future.

On the grounds that their father seemed to need their full support at present, she decided to say nothing for the moment. But she got up and helped Josy clear the table, growing more and more aware that, while support him she would, once this crisis at Fereday Products was resolved, she was going to take Josy from under his roof and find somewhere else to live.

'Do you think you should ring him now?' Josy asked anxiously, once everything had been tidied up.

Had it been up to her she would never ring him, so why, when it was not for herself, did her insides feel like so much jelly as she dialled his number and waited, and waited? 'He's not in,' she reported to her sister, while trying to hide the mixed emotions she felt about that.

Suddenly though, just as she was about to put down the phone, an unmistakably all-male voice said, 'Hello,' in her ear—and her insides went all of a tremble.

'Oh, hello,' she answered, relieved to find that her voice sounded remarkably light. 'I was beginning to think you weren't in.'

'What can I do for you?' he asked, apparently recognising her voice at once, for he did not ask her who it was.

'I—um...' God, she felt all of a lather. 'I wondered if you'd like to come to dinner on Saturday.' She pulled herself sharply together and got the invitation out—and had to wait an agonising number of embarrassed seconds while he chewed her invitation over.

'Let me get this straight,' he queried, as if he was not quite comprehending what she had said, when she knew full well he had been at the forefront of the queue when intelligence had been given out, 'you're asking me to dine with you this coming Saturday?'

Say no, she silently begged, say you've got a previous engagement. 'My family would like you to dine with us— I'm their spokeswoman,' she replied, hoping he'd use some of that vast supply of intelligence she had credited him with to realise that for herself she'd starve rather than sit at the same table with him ever again.

'Josy—if she's better—she'll be there?'

Most peculiarly, Belvia found his question had reached her sense of humour. 'Er—if she's better,' she agreed.

'And—what about you?'

'Me?'

'I understood you were having an affair with a married man?'

There was suddenly such a toughness in his tone that Belvia at that moment knew that anyone who ever crossed this man would live to regret it. But she banished such thoughts. She had not crossed him—well, not to any great degree, anyhow—and, to get back to his statement, she guessed she only had herself to blame that he thought she was having an affair. Had she not said in front of him last Friday—flippantly into the bargain— that after dinner was the only time her date could get away from his wife?

She could, Belvia supposed, have owned up that she was not involved with any married man. But Latham Tavenner seemed to bring out the worst in her—and instead she found herself stating, 'I cancelled my date for Saturday when my father said it would be more agreeable for you if we were four at dinner.'

'You shouldn't have cancelled your date on my account,' he retorted sharply. 'You must have enough restrictions on the time available to meet your lover behind his wife's back.'

'That's true!' she retaliated, then caught sight of Josy, looking at her as if to say she was not going about getting him to accept her invitation in a very polite tone. But by then Belvia was well and truly upset by one Latham Tavenner, and demanded, 'Are you coming or not?'

'Get your sister to give me a ring!' he snarled—Belvia had an idea that they both slammed down the phone at the same time.

For two seconds more she fumed about the ghastly rattlesnake of a man—and then became aware of Josy watching her, all large-eyed and fearing the worst. Belvia forgot her anger with the financier to tell her, 'I—blew it!'

'Oh, heavens—Father will be livid! What did Mr Tavenner say?'

How to tell her? There was no way, Belvia realised, in which she could dress it up. 'He—wants you to phone him,' she said in a rush. And, as Josy lost some of the little colour she had, 'But you don't have to,' she told her firmly.

Josy stared at her and, Belvia realised, was patently remembering their father's attitude, his anger over dinner, and, 'Yes, I do,' she answered quietly.

'Well, not tonight you don't,' Belvia stated quickly, even as she said it wondering if she was right to get her sister to put off making a phone call that to anyone else might be a simple phone call, but which just thinking about would give her sister nightmares. 'Although it might be better out of the way.'

'I'll sleep on it,' Josy replied, clearly shrinking from having anything to do with the self-assured man.

Belvia was hating Latham Tavenner with a vengeance as she lay sleepless in her bed that night. When, however, fairness tried to nudge its honest way in—it was hardly his fault because, but for the Feredays needing to keep him sweet because they were after his money, they need have nothing to do with him—Belvia ousted such unwanted honesty. He *was* at fault. Of course, he had no idea of the dreadful tragedy that had befallen Josy when her husband had been killed, but that did not make it any better. He must have seen for himself how withdrawn Josy was before Belvia had told him of her sister's extreme shyness. Yet now he was waiting for Josy to telephone him—he wanted hanging up by his ears!

At that moment visions of Latham Tavenner's quite nice ears sprang into Belvia's mind out of nowhere—as, too, did a remembered image of his good-looking, if arrogant, face. Good grief, she fumed, and buried her head under the bedclothes—as if to escape him.

But there was no escape from him the next day. It started at breakfast. 'Did you ring Latham Tavenner last night?' her father asked, when she had barely sat down at the breakfast-table.

'I did.'

'And?'

Belvia avoided looking at her sister. 'Nothing's been settled yet.' Her father was waiting for more. 'But it will be before dinner-time on Saturday.'

'See that it is,' he grunted, then finished his breakfast in stony silence, and left for his office.

'You might like to give thought to you and me moving out from this house—once Father's got his loan,' Belvia blurted out to Josy, this time too upset by her father's manner to hold her thoughts back.

'I couldn't do that!' Josy gasped.

'You know, you could, love,' Belvia argued gently. 'We could find a small flat somewhere, and——'

'But what about Father—who'd look after him?'

'He's big enough to look after himself, and, if he isn't, he can jolly well pay a housekeeper.'

'I—couldn't, Bel—not now...'

'Well, don't fret about it. It was just an idea.' Belvia smiled—and hoped that, now the idea had been planted, perhaps as the days and weeks went on her sister might grow to the idea.

It was early afternoon when Belvia went up to the stables to exercise Hetty. She had said not a word to Josy about the fact that there was a phone call to one Latham Tavenner outstanding, but toyed seriously with the notion of dialling his number and saying that her sister had been called away for a few days and had asked her to ring. She would say that Josy would be back by Saturday, she decided, warming to the idea, and then again ask him to dinner.

She had it all worked out by the time she had returned home, and went looking for Josy. She found her in the sitting-room—and one look at her face was enough to tell her that something was wrong.

'What's happened?' she asked, going quickly over to her.

'I rang him.'

Belvia did not need two guesses. 'At his work?' she enquired, realising that it must have taken a great deal of courage for Josy to do that.

'I thought I was leaving much too much to you, so I...'

'Oh, love,' Belvia murmured.

'Anyhow, to be honest, it was with the bright idea in my head that if I rang Latham Tavenner at his office, he wouldn't have time to take my call and I could leave a message to say I'd rung, and...'

'And you'd be absolved from ringing him again?' Belvia took up.

'Only it wasn't such a bright idea as I thought it was, because after his PA had taken my name he came on the line—and I nearly died.'

'Never mind—you did it, and it's all over now,' Belvia comforted. Somehow, though, she saw no relief in Josy's expression that, her call made, she could forget about him until Saturday. 'Was he very much of a brute to you?' she asked, sorely wanting to set about him.

'No, not really. In fact, I suppose you could say that, given he was firm, his tone was quite kind.'

Kind! She would never associate him with 'kind'! 'Er—what was he firm about?' Belvia asked, a little puzzled. 'You mean he gave you a firm yes about coming to dinner on Saturday?'

Josy shook her lovely head. 'He was firm about not coming here to dinner,' she replied, her voice starting to break, 'but he suggested, since I'd cooked dinner for him the last time, that I must go to his place for dinner this time.'

'You're not going!' In a flash Belvia was up in arms, whether her sister thought she was going or not, making that decision for her. 'No way are you going!' she added forcefully.

'But, Bel, I've got to. You heard Father...'

'You've got to do nothing of the sort!' Belvia would not hear of it, and as she began to cope with the initial shock of Latham Tavenner's invitation to her sister continued, 'Was the invitation for you alone? Not you and Father?' she queried, not needing to enquire if she was excluded—that was a foreknown fact.

'Just me. He made that plain. I shall have to go!' Josy cried in panic. 'If I don't, Father will have to close down, and all those people will be put out of work, and——'

'And leave it with me. I'll think of something,' Belvia promised—and had until Saturday to come up with something brilliant.

*   *   *

By Saturday their father had been acquainted with the fact that Josy had been invited to dine with Latham Tavenner in his London flat. Edwin Fereday seemed much pleased by this news—so much so that, for the moment, and in the interests of a pleasant home-life, Belvia thought it better not to disillusion him. Latham Tavenner had suggested he would send a car for Josy, but she had said she would drive herself. But, Belvia fumed, over her dead body would Josy be dining with him alone in his flat or with him anywhere else.

Though how to get her out of it? Belvia thought up plenty of ideas, but none which could not be overcome. Josy's car could break down—Latham would send a car for her. Belvia thought perhaps she could ring him and say that it really was not on for him to expect Josy when she had told him herself of her extreme shyness—to which of course he might answer, 'Fine,' which would mean that not only would they never see or hear from him again but—immediately losing his 'in' with him—neither would their father.

'I shall have to go,' Josy said worriedly after lunch on Saturday.

Belvia did not need to ask, Go where? 'Where' was to the forefront of both their minds. 'I've told you you're not going,' she reiterated, and remembering that, although Josy was terrified of him, she had thought him kind, Belvia realised her only hope lay in hoping Josy had got that bit right—she would appeal to his kindness. 'I've decided to give him a ring and to ask if he'll see me. Then I'll explain that because—because you've recently suffered a great sadness in your——'

'You won't tell him about Marc!' Josy exclaimed, tears rushing to her eyes.

'Oh, love, would you mind so much?' In an instant Belvia was by her side, an arm about her shoulders.

'He'd tell Father—I couldn't take him ridiculing...'

'Shh, it's all right, don't worry.' Belvia calmed her. To her mind it had seemed a good, if not the only, option. If Latham had half the honour he was said to possess, then surely he would be appalled to know that he was not just trying to get on better terms with a very attractive woman, but was in fact causing more distress to an already distressed and grieving widow. 'I'll ring him anyway and ask if he'd mind seeing me,' Belvia determined.

'With what in mind?'

Belvia tried to bring all the confidence which she was far from feeling into her smile. And, having already told Latham Tavenner of her sister's shyness, she stated, 'I'll impress on him how shy you are, how—um—difficult you find it to make new friends.'

'Do you think that will be enough?'

'We can give it a try,' Belvia replied brightly. 'Somehow I'll get him to leave you alone.' She went at once to the phone and dialled—and found he was not in.

From then she rang his number every half-hour, but there was still no reply. Damn him, she started to fume. As someone expecting a dinner guest that evening, he should at this very moment be slaving away over a hot stove!

Suddenly the minute hand on the clock seemed fairly to race round. Belvia tried Latham Tavenner's number once more and knew, when there was again no reply, that she had only one option left. She, as she had done before, was going to have to turn up, unwanted and unasked, in her sister's place. She went upstairs to bath and change.

'I feel dreadful letting you do this for me,' Josy fretted when, with Belvia already running late, she went out to the car with her.

'Just keep out of Father's way if he comes home early—which I doubt. He'll never know which one of us went.' Belvia smiled, and started up her car—her insides filled with dread. She did not need a barrow-load of premonition to know that there would be no welcome awaiting her.

With her thoughts varied—frequently panicky, less frequently calm—she somehow made it without mishap to the impressive building where Latham Tavenner had his apartment. And, having parked her car, she entered the well-lighted building to find her way blocked by a uniformed commissionaire.

'I've an engagement with Mr Tavenner,' she smiled prettily to tell him.

He had seen it all before, and smiled back. 'May I have your name, madam?'

'Fereday. B... Miss Fereday.'

Her insides were behaving no better than they had been before when she sailed up in the lift and got out where she had been directed. Oh, how she wished that this were all over and that she was on her way back home!

She found his door, rang the bell, and waited to be annihilated.

She was not far wrong. The door opened and he stood there, tall, sophisticated, casually clad—and disbelieving. Indeed, so disbelieving was he that while her voice died in her throat he took a step past her into the hall, as if to check for himself that, incredibly, it looked as if she had again come in her sister's stead.

'Where's Josy?' he demanded, clearly unimpressed as his eyes took in her shoulder-length shining blonde hair and her slender shape in a simple, classic, light wool dress of deepest lavender.

'She—er...' Her voice faded.

'I don't believe this!' he snarled, and to her consternation seemed about to close the door on her.

'I can explain!' Belvia burst out quickly.

He halted. 'I was expecting your sister an hour ago!' he rapped pointedly.

'She did try to ring!' Belvia lied desperately. 'Only you weren't in.' Not a smile, not a glimmer of any softening. 'I lost my way,' she added to her lie total. 'I'm sorry I'm late,' she offered appeasingly.

'I wasn't expecting *you*!' he emphasised.

And Josy had imagined he was kind! Belvia started to get cross, even while she knew that she could not afford the luxury. Then she remembered how this brute of a man had said that he treated a woman as she deserved to be treated. 'Can I come in?' she asked bluntly. Unmistakably, this swine had seen that Josy deserved a kind tone. Belvia knew for sure that she would never get that luxury.

'I'm going to eat!' he informed her curtly.

'I haven't had my dinner either,' she dared, and guessed she was about to be flattened for her sauce. But, miraculously, she saw his lips twitch in the way that they had that time she had mistakenly thought she had amused him. He was not amused this time either, though, she saw, when his mouth suddenly looked not at all like smiling. 'I wanted to explain—about Josy,' she added in a rush, when it still looked as if he might close the door on her—this thing had to be settled *now*.

'Is it going to take long?'

It could do; she had not a clue what she could tell him without bringing Marc into it. 'I'll be as brief as I can,' she promised—and did not know if she was relieved or otherwise when he relented and stood back from the door to allow her into his apartment.

'You'd better share my meal,' he grunted unenthusiastically.

As long as you don't put arsenic on my share, she thought sweetly, and entered a thickly carpeted sitting-room that was roomy enough to house half a dozen settees, but in actual fact housed only two, plus a few well-padded chairs and low antique tables.

'We'll go straight through to the dining-room,' her hungry, unwilling host stated, leading the way.

'Er, could I wash my hands first?' she enquired, as she desperately sought for time to find a way to tell him, tactfully, to leave her sister alone.

Latham threw her a look which she read as one of regret that he had agreed to let her in. 'Second on the right, through there,' he grunted, and left her to it.

Her mind was much the same blank as it had been when, ten minutes later, she joined him in the dining-room. There were two places laid at the highly polished table, and he was standing by one of them.

She gave him full marks that, despite his annoyance to find he was again feeding her, he waited until she was seated before taking his own seat. She picked up her knife and cut into a portion of pâté which obviously came from a high-class delicatessen.

'Mmm, this is good,' she murmured, all wide brown eyes. 'Did you make it yourself?'

Again she saw that minuscule movement of his fabulous mouth. But, as before, any suggestion of a smile didn't make it. 'You know bloody well I didn't,' he growled.

'Oh,' she mumbled, and knew that she had better watch her step. Another comment like that and he would be slinging her out before she'd had a chance to get through to him about Josy. Josy—think about Josy. Josy was why she was here. Belvia drew herself up short—how on earth had it come about that she could so far forget about Josy as to think that this man who terrified the poor love had a fabulous mouth! 'Mr Tavenner,' she said in a rush—and became aware on that instant that, surprisingly for such a hungry man, he had not been eating, but had been studying her for quite a few seconds. That realisation made her forget whatever it was she had been about to say.

Nor did she have any chance of remembering either when, quite out of the blue, he remarked, 'You're so beautiful.' She stared at him, barely believing her ears. Nor could she believe—his statement on her beauty had been so matter-of-fact—that he should follow it up with a churlish, 'Why the hell, with all you've got going for you, do you have to snare yourself up with a married man?'

Belvia supposed it must have been because she was still stunned that he had paid her a compliment, no matter how matter-of-factly put, that she did not at once deny that she had any liaison with a married man. In fact, she was sure she must have stared at him in shock for a full five seconds before the last of what he said made sense in her brain. 'Mr Tavenner,' she began.

But his churlishness had given way to mockery. 'Mr Tavenner—twice?' he drawled, as if to remind her that she had called him Latham when he had phoned on Tuesday afternoon.

'Are you suggesting I use your first name?'

'I'm suggesting you eat your pâté. There's a casserole in the oven drying up.'

Belvia was glad of the respite from having to launch into her 'hands off my sister' campaign. For good manners decreed she could not speak with her mouth full.

The casserole was not dried up, and tasted delicious. 'This never came out of any delicatessen,' she murmured appreciatively. 'Nor,' she added, knowing it for certain, 'did you make it.'

'There are other things I'm better at,' he admitted, which left her wondering if one of his lady-friends had served time in his kitchen. That thought disturbed her. She most definitely did not like that thought—though she could not think of one possible reason why she did not. Nor why she should feel immediately better when Latham added, 'My daily is also a genius in the kitchen.' So his cleaning-lady had made it for him. 'Wine?' he enquired.

'I'm driving,' she refused, wanting to keep a clear head, and smiled, then saw his glance on her smiling, upturned mouth.

His mouth, however, when she was somehow irresistibly drawn to stare at it, had never been more unsmiling. In fact, when she raised her eyes and met the granite grey of his arctic look, she knew that his mood

had changed yet again. She was not, therefore, totally
unprepared for his hostility when he snarled, 'So keen
to stay within the drink-drive laws that you abstain totally
when driving! What a pity you don't hold the laws of
marriage in such high regard.'

'What on earth are you talking about?' she gasped.

'Spare me!' he thundered, his expression taut and
menacing as he leaned towards her, his jaw jutting at an
aggressive angle. 'You've already admitted to having an
adulterous relationship.'

'No, I . . .' she began. 'Well, I . . .'

'Strange, I thought you could lie all the time!' he
grated, manifestly not taken by her amending her 'no'
to a prevarication.

'So I've lied—a little,' she had to admit.

'At every chance you've had, I'd say . . .'

'Listen, you!' she snapped, suddenly enraged. She did
not have to sit here and take this. Her meal was forgotten in her fury, everything forgotten as, eyes flashing,
she shot to her feet, slamming her napkin down. 'If I've
lied to you, it's been for good——'

'If? Ye gods!' he scorned.

'For good reason! And about having an affair
with——'

He was on his feet too, and, just as she was wishing
he was nearer so that she could ease her itching palm by
belting him one, he had moved, and in a couple of strides
he was standing directly in front of her.

But her urge to set about him physically was denied
her when, his fury suddenly matching hers, he caught
hold of her by her upper arms—making her powerless
to get a swing in at him—and roared, 'Don't lie to me
about that!'

'What?'

'About sleeping around—careless of whether he's got a married label att——'

'How dare you?' she erupted. 'I don't sleep around. I——'

'You'll be telling me next you're a virgin!'

'And you wouldn't believe that either!'

'You're damned right I wouldn't believe it.'

'Then to hell with you!' she exploded, and turned to leave—and found that he still had hold of her, refusing to let her go. The result of her fast, halted action caused her to stumble against him. 'Get away from me!' she shrieked, outraged, and gave him a push which, violent as it was, moved him not an inch.

She glared up into the blaze of fury in his fierce grey eyes, and her heart almost stopped at the intent she saw there. 'My God, when did you get to be so fussy?' he sneered cuttingly, and in the next split second the hands that had been on her arms were like iron bands about her, pinning her arms to her sides, and the split second after that, for all she tried to jerk her head out of the way, his mouth had found hers in a savage, angry kiss.

'*No!*' she screamed, the moment he took his mouth from hers. It was as much time as she had before he claimed her mouth again.

With what freedom of movement she did have she pushed frantically to try and break free, but he would not let her go. In fact, all she succeeded in doing was to make him hold her more firmly to him. She could feel his body, his warmth, and his strength. It scared her, made her own strength seem puny.

That fear made her fight the harder. She tried desperately to kick at his shins, but did not connect. She

twisted and turned her body in an attempt to be free—
and found that by wriggling up against him she had
earned herself more savage kisses.

'Keep that up, sweetheart, and we might have a lot of
fun.'

'Stuff your promises!' she returned spiritedly, and
gasped as, this time, instead of his mouth coming over
hers again, he opted to trail kisses down the side of her
throat.

She swallowed convulsively, realising that, while she
was still in a dangerous situation, she somehow no longer
felt so threatened as she had! Although still panicking,
she was in charge of that panic. Sufficiently at any rate
for her to realise that if her violent movements against
him to be free seemed to be inciting him to passion then
she must have the nerve to stay passive.

She had nothing to lose, she felt—when another un-
successful attempt to be free only gave him the chance
to pull her to him—and everything to gain. She might,
by staying passive in his arms, get him to let go his steely
hold on her a little. Enough, anyhow, for her to find a
chance to scrape her foot down his shin—that should
make him hop a bit, and so would she—right out of
there.

On that instant, before she could think of it further,
Belvia stopped struggling. To her surprise, it worked!
For instantly Latham leaned back from her and, while
still holding her in the circle of his arms, stared down
into her face. And then he smiled, a smile which she
afterwards realised she should not have believed in. But
it was the first smile he had shown her personally, and
she was so shaken by it that, while still in the grip of
surprise that he was no longer forcing himself on her,

she forgot entirely her intention to scrape a few layers of skin off his shin.

And then it was too late. Because, as his hold on her all at once gentled, suddenly his head was coming down and, tenderly this time, Latham laid his mouth over hers in an all-giving kiss, and Belvia was lost. Never had she known such a beautiful kiss. Never had she known a kiss could be so beautiful.

'Latham!' she whispered when he broke that kiss, her world upside-down. She stared up at him and he stared back down into her receptive wide brown eyes.

She had no idea what signals she was giving off, but with her heart beating as it had never beaten before, she had not the smallest objection to make when his head came down and, gently, he claimed her mouth again. She moved her arms and found them free, and was glad, because she was then able to put them around him.

And it was bliss, pure bliss. He held her firmly, but without force. With expert fingers he slid the zip at the back of her neck down a little way, and she was entirely unaware that he had done so until she felt his warm, mobile, fabulous mouth kissing the nakedness of her shoulders.

She clutched on to him. She was not very sure about this. His mouth returned to claim hers, and she felt she had nothing to worry about. While his wonderful mouth still held hers, though, she felt his fingers caressing inside her unzipped dress at the back. And again she gripped on to him when warm, sensitive fingers caressed her shoulder, sliding her bra-strap to one side.

Then all at once emotions she had never dreamed of were licking into life inside her. She was conscious, vaguely, that as they kissed they moved. She had thought—while acknowledging that she was not thinking very clearly—that they had moved only a yard or so. But, when she opened her eyes from yet another gentle onslaught to her senses, she found that they were standing at an open bedroom door.

Her heart was thundering against her ribs. This was not right; she knew it was not right. Yet Latham had so awakened her senses that what was right and what was wrong were hazy. All she knew was that she did not want it to stop.

Yet somewhere, something was holding her back, 'Th-this is as far as I go,' she managed chokily, and felt she did not hate him after all, but really liked him when he smiled a wonderful smile.

'That decision is all yours, beautiful Belvia,' he murmured. 'Though—perhaps—one last kiss?'

What a wonderful suggestion—she would have felt bereft without another, just one last kiss. She smiled willingly, and he read her answer in that willing smile. And what a kiss it was! Belvia had thought she had learned a lot that night about the different quality there could be in a kiss. But as Latham's head came down once more and he pulled her slender body close up to him again yet another dimension was added, and as passion between them soared higher she went with him without protest through that open bedroom door.

'Do you want me?' he asked, teasing her lips apart with his.

'Oh, yes,' she breathed, aching for him—and abruptly hit terra firma with the cruellest of jolts.

For one minute she was in his arms—willing, eager to be taught everything he could teach her—and the next she was standing alone. Totally alone and isolated, for all that Latham was not a yard away from her. Feeling utterly bewildered, she stared at him, doing her best to comprehend that there was a look about him that seemed to say that he had not the smallest interest whatsoever in making her his.

'What...?' she gasped. 'I...' But, taking in his look of sheer mockery, she seemed totally unable to string two words together.

'What an actress!' he drawled, not a glimmer about him of a man wanting desperately to make love. Indeed, his look toughened, his tone became grating as he went on to gibe, 'And you say you don't sleep around?'

Her mouth fell open in utter shock. But she was not thinking or feeling as shock gave way to rage. A rage of rejection consumed her. A rage that came from being made to look a fool, being gibed at, stormed in and took total charge of her. He had been leading her on! He had been leading her on so that he could gibe, sneer, and throw back at her, 'And you say you don't sleep around!'

Never had Belvia been so almighty furious as when, taking a fierce step closer so as to be certain not to miss, she yelled, 'Not around here, sweetheart!' and hurled a blow across his face which almost sprained her wrist.

There was still a red mist in front of her eyes when she turned and went smartly out of there, with only the satisfactory, painful stinging in her right hand to tell her that indeed she had not missed, but had found her target—dead on.

CHAPTER FOUR

BELVIA woke early on Sunday morning after a fractured night's sleep. Oh, Lord, it seemed worse with the coming of daylight rather than better, as she had hoped.

Had that really been her last night? The wanton, the pugilist? She winced in her bed, still stunned by her behaviour, and never wanted to get up. Oh, grief, what was happening to her? Before she had met Latham Tavenner she had been an even-tempered and, for the most part, logical-thinking female. Yet, since knowing him, everything she knew about herself, or thought she knew about herself, had been turned upside-down!

She would have liked to think that it was all his fault. That had he not kissed her so expertly, touched her skin so tenderly, she would not have responded as she had. But she had been kissed pretty near expertly before— and had never come close to losing her head.

She heard Josy moving about in the room next door and, feeling impatient with herself, she jumped out of bed and headed for the shower. Josy, she knew, would be anxious to know how she had got on. Indeed, she had been waiting up for her last night, but her father had followed her in, and Josy had made herself scarce before he had a chance to see her.

Belvia owned that she had been glad of the respite, though she had no more idea now than she had had then of what she was going to tell her. The whole point of her going to see Latham had been to find some way of making him see he should leave his pursuit of her sister—yet not a word to him had she said in that direction.

Belvia came from the bathroom knowing that there was no way she was going to tell her sister any of what had taken place last night. How, when her intention at the outset had been to keep him sweet, she had landed him one and stormed out of his flat—doing up her dress as she descended in the lift.

Her cheeks grew hot as thoughts that had racked her through the night assaulted her again now. Would she, after years of instinctively knowing that she would give herself only when love was there, have given herself to Latham Tavenner—this man she hated? That he had called a halt before it had got that far was academic; it was herself, her own reactions, which were crucifying her.

Though what about him? Josy was the one he was after, not her. Belvia admitted that her physical and sexual knowledge of the opposite sex was limited but, even so, she was not so green that she could not tell when a man wanted her, even if he did have such control over his sexual urges that he could suppress his wanting—and reject her.

Was she greener than she had thought, anyhow? Had he not wanted her after all, but been more intent on proving that her 'I don't sleep around' claim was the rot he believed it was? Swine. She started to grow angry again. She was glad she had belted him. Then she remembered her father, and how he was desperate to do business with Latham, and she gave a groan of despair. Then she heard a light tap on her door, and Josy came in.

'Hello, Jo,' Belvia greeted her brightly. 'You're up early.'

'So are you,' Josy commented, and, as Belvia knew she would, 'How did it go?' she asked worriedly.

And that was where Belvia knew that, even if she had to lie her head off, she was going to make sure that Josy had one day in which she was not going to be plagued with anxiety. 'Fine,' she smiled.

'You were able to convince him that he's wasting his time with me?' Josy pressed, and Belvia knew that her twin would not just be unable to cope but would be terrified if ever Latham took her in his arms as he had her last night.

'As you noticed, he has a very kind streak in him.' Like hell he did! 'He gave me dinner, and was very understanding—about you being shy, I mean. He asked me to give you his best wishes.' Belvia thought that should do it—any more and it might be over the top.

'And—he won't be phoning here any more?'

If she prevaricated, Josy would worry. 'No,' she replied positively, and determined to stand guard by the phone all week.

Fortunately their father seemed to have other matters on his mind and forgot to ask how Josy had got on with the financier at dinner the previous evening. Belvia later heard him on the phone arranging to spend the day with a lady-friend, and Sunday passed without anything happening to ruffle the calmer waters Belvia thought her sister was sailing in.

For the rest of the week that followed Belvia managed to make all the right responses whenever her father mentioned Latham Tavenner, which, as chance had it, seemed to be only when Josy was not around. For that week too, Belvia stayed close to the phone whenever she could. Because Josy might wonder why she was not exercising Hetty, if she followed through her fleeting idea to pay the stables to exercise her, Belvia went each afternoon to attend the horse. Each time she dashed home, though, it was to see that, given that everything was wrong with Josy's world, she was starting to look more and more relaxed as the week went by.

When Sunday rolled around again and not a word had Josy heard from Latham Tavenner, Belvia began to wonder if he had given up his pursuit of her sister.

Evidence, however, that he had by no means given up that pursuit came only a few hours later. Their father had not come home the previous night, and she and Josy were having a cup of coffee in the sitting-room when the phone rang. How she could have allowed herself to become so complacent Belvia could not explain. Though perhaps it was because she had been so keyed up all week, expecting Latham to ring, that, when he had not, she had started to believe that he would not—not now. Which was why, Josy being the nearer to the phone, she let her answer it.

'Hello?' said Josy, and went ashen.

In a flash, instinct screaming at her who was on the phone, Belvia was out of her chair and grabbing the phone out of her sister's hand. 'Hello!' she gasped.

Silence. Then, 'I was talking to Josy!' Latham Tavenner stated harshly. Oh, grief, he hadn't forgiven her for attempting to break his jaw, then—not that she had expected him to.

'I'm sorry,' she murmured politely, unsure if she was being polite for his sake, for Josy's sake—whom she would have believe she had nothing to worry about—or for her father's sake, not to mention his employees'. 'Josy had to dash off. She's got something burning in the oven.' She saw a look of relief wash over Josy's face, and smiled encouragingly and nodded when she saw her sister stack the coffee-tray and indicate that she was going to take their used coffee-cups to the kitchen.

'We can't have your Sunday roast cindered,' Latham offered sarcastically, and Belvia knew that he hadn't believed her excuse for a minute.

She waited to answer until Josy had closed the sitting-room door behind her. This was dreadful! She had thought... 'What did you want Josy for?' she asked abruptly.

'Please,' he suggested, reminding her of her manners.

My God, he was doing it again, making her want to thump him! Never had she met a man who could so effortlessly upset her equilibrium. She swallowed hard, and rephrased her question. 'What can we do for you?' she enquired, trying to make her voice as pleasant as possible.

'We?'

Her right hand itched. 'Me, then,' she pushed out from between clenched teeth.

'You don't consider you've done—enough?'

Oh, my... She struggled to stay calm. 'I consider that, when I b—— hit you on Saturday, you had it coming. Which,' she tacked on swiftly, 'if you're half as honourable as they say you are, you'll admit is——'

'Don't you dare talk to me about honour!' he clipped.

Oh, hell, he was off again about that affair she had made out she was having with a married man. Now did not seem to be the time to renew her denial. 'So we're both in the wrong.' She swallowed down impetuous words to get him to think better of her—grief, as if she cared! 'Um, Latham.' Damn, now why had his name just slipped out? Crazy. 'The thing is, it looks as if Josy's having a few problems in the kitchen—she really did go to the kitchen—er—can I take a message for you?'

Silence. Frantically, if belatedly, Belvia tried desperately for something to say that would retrieve a situation that looked to be rushing headlong into 'Who needs the Feredays anyway?' That might be marvellous for Josy, but would be ruinous for her father.

'It was your sister I wanted to speak to,' he stated at last. 'I hear she's pretty good about horse-flesh—I'd value her opinion on a horse I'm thinking of buying.'

And if I believe that I'll believe anything, Belvia fumed, knowing full well that if he wanted an opinion on horse-flesh he would go directly to the top expert. But she was feeling sick inside that all too clearly Latham's pursuit of Josy had never let up. Most probably he had been out of town on business this week—and this was his first chance... She took a shaky breath as she suddenly realised that she was going to have to do what she should have done a week ago, what she had gone to his flat to do, in fact—appeal to his better nature, if he had one.

'Look, Latham,' she began, her tone conciliatory.

'Oh, you're still there!'

Sarcastic swine. Did he think she had rushed off to drag Josy back to the phone? 'The thing is...' She hesitated, no more ready now with what she wanted to say than she had been before.

'Yes?' he prompted.

'Well...' She took a deep breath. 'Can I see you?' she plunged.

A dreadful silence followed her blunt request, during which she felt quite mortified. For herself, she would never ask. For Josy, she had to ask—even if it meant she had put herself on the receiving end of a ton of sarcasm for her trouble.

'You—want a return match?' he asked finally, and Belvia knew he was referring to the way she had put all her slender weight behind the blow she had struck him.

'No,' she replied quietly, so that he would know that it was not her usual habit to resort to physical violence— though, come to think of it, no one of her acquaintance earned it the way he did.

'You're saying—that you want a date?' he asked incredulously, deliberately misunderstanding her, she was sure. 'You're asking me to go out with you?'

'No, I'm *not*!' She blew it in no uncertain fashion, her aggressiveness out in the open. Who in creation did he think he was? she seethed, not mistaking that tone in his voice which clearly showed he was not one bit enamoured of the idea of a date with her. But she bit down her ire. 'I need to talk to you—to explain about...'

'Josy,' he finished for her. 'You didn't make a very good job of it last time,' he did not hesitate to remind her.

Rodent! she smouldered, wanting only to forget the whole of that 'last time'. Only, clearly, he was not going to let her. 'Please,' she swallowed her pride to utter— and again had to wait while he thought the matter over.

'I could give you lunch, I suppose,' he thought out loud. Today? What the dickens would she wear? 'But I don't see why I should.' Pig, she fumed, hating him afresh and starting to believe he was playing some cat-and-mouse game with her for his own amusement. There was nothing in any way remotely amused in his tone, however, when after a moment more of consideration he told her decisively, 'You know where I live—come here tonight.'

Belvia stared in disbelief at the dead phone in her hand. The misbegotten brute—he'd put the phone down on her!

A minute later and she was still finding fresh names for him. It had always been her prerogative to say yea or nay, but he, the monster, had just taken that prerogative away from her and, because of Josy, she could do nothing about it.

Thinking of her sister reminded her that Josy would be nervously waiting to hear what that phone call had been all about. And that was when Belvia accepted that, for quite some while now, because of Josy, because of their father, her yea or nay where Latham Tavenner was concerned had been immaterial. He stated, made his wishes known, and she had to comply.

Belvia tilted her chin at a defiant angle. So be it. She went in search of Josy facing that, because she had no choice; she would have to put up with being bossed around by Mr Come-here-tonight, End-of-conversation. She would go because she had to, because she would do anything she had to to end this particular torment for Josy—but, oh, how she wished she need never have anything more to do with him.

'What did he want?' Josy wanted to know the moment she saw her.

'Nothing to get stewed up about,' Belvia smiled. 'He'd merely heard, from Father probably, that you knew horse-flesh, and he wanted your opinion on a horse he's thinking of buying.'

'You told him I no longer have anything to do with horses?' Josy asked urgently.

'Of course. Don't be upset. I told you you had nothing to worry about with Latham, didn't I?' Belvia went on cheerily. 'Which you'd have discovered for yourself if I hadn't been such an idiot and grabbed the phone from you,' she laughed.

Belvia was not laughing later when, in the early evening, she began to feel extremely agitated about seeing Latham again. Oh, for goodness' sake. She tried impatiently to snap herself out of it. What could happen to her that had not happened to her already?

Because of her inner agitation, though, she dressed with special care, as if hoping her red short-sleeved crêpe dress would give her some confidence.

'You didn't say you were going out,' Josy remarked when she popped her head round the sitting-room door.

'I just thought I'd drive over and see Kate, in case she's feeling a bit lost since her retirement.' And, playing her ace, 'Would you like to come?' Josy had never met Kate; her answer was a foregone conclusion.

'No, thanks,' Josy smiled.

'See you, then. Shouldn't be too late—well, not unless Kate's starved for company and wants to talk late.'

Belvia did not hurry. While she was anxious for this meeting to be over, she was not so anxious to meet Latham again. She was not hungry and had no mind to share his dinner this time, so deliberately made sure that she did not enter the foyer of his apartments before nine.

The same commissionaire was on duty as before. 'Good evening, Miss Fereday,' he greeted her, and as he went over to the lifts with her and pressed the appropriate button Belvia understood how he had got his job.

Commissionaires did not come any more alert, tactful and smart than this man.

Her thoughts were all on another man, the man she was there to see, well before the lift stopped at his floor. With her insides churning, she walked along to his door and pressed the bell.

He kept her waiting, and that niggled her, and she was glad to feel niggled. Given that she was there to appeal to his better nature, she felt better able to cope with how she was feeling as she experienced a spurt of annoyance.

Then she heard him coming to the door, and her insides were aflutter again. The door opened, and he stood there, as she remembered him, dark-haired, grey-eyed, and cool with it. He was casually dressed in shirt and trousers, 'Come in,' he invited, his eyes taking in her blonde hair framing her face, her neatly fitting dress. 'I'm just finishing my meal.' She pinned a pleasant look on her face and went in. 'You can make some coffee,' he stated—it sounded like an order. Her pleasant look started to slip. Oh, for some rat-poison!

'I think I know where the kitchen is,' she murmured as evenly as she could and, to cover that she would prefer to punch his head, she went kitchenwards.

In the kitchen she found the makings for his coffee and, to the devil with it, found two cups and set to work making coffee and trying to restore her equilibrium. With him so close, it somehow was not easy, and she loaded a tray, working hard on an entry line. How's business? No, she couldn't say that! Latham Tavenner was a shrewd operator. She did not want to give him the smallest cause to associate her visit in any way with business—her father would be furious if she slipped up and gave away the smallest clue that he would not mind doing business with Latham. Her father always had played his cards close to his chest.

She carried the tray into the dining-room—only to find that Latham had transferred to the sitting-room. He took the tray from her when she went in, and set it down on a small table in front of a well-padded, luxurious couch.

'Have you lived here long?' She looked about as she offered an everyday question.

'Some while,' he replied, indicating she should take a seat on the couch. 'It's a useful base,' he commented.

Belvia did as he indicated and sat herself behind the coffee-pot—and at once felt her equilibrium slip when Latham opted to sit on the couch beside her. 'You're not here all the time, then?' she enquired, her brain picking that up from what he had just said while she tried to get the rest of her act together.

'I'm frequently away,' he agreed.

'You've been away this week?' She followed through her thought of earlier that day, that he had been out of town on business that week.

'I flew in this morning,' he confirmed.

Not merely out of town, but out of the country by the sound of it! It did not bode well for her sister, Belvia considered, that one of the first things he did on his return was to pick up the phone and ring Josy on the pretext of asking her about some horse he was interested in.

She poured him a cup of coffee, aware that she was skirting around the real issue of why she was there. 'Cream?' she enquired.

'Black, thanks,' he answered, and then, when she was mentally getting her words in order to talk of Josy, he upset her concentration by asking abruptly, 'Where's the boyfriend tonight?'

'There isn't one,' she replied, and saw his brow darken.

'You never felt it necessary to lie about his existence before!' he reminded her sharply, and Belvia realised the situation was going rapidly downhill—not at all the way it was supposed to go.

'Oh, that...' she began but, looking at him, she saw from the cold look in his grey eyes that things had gone too far for her to try now to convince him that there was not any married lover in her life. To try to convince him, she realised, would only make it seem she was protesting too much, and convince him of the opposite. Anyway, she thought, starting to feel niggled again, why should she try to convince him of anything to do with her? It was not why she was here. She placed her coffee-cup back on the table. 'Do you mind if we talk about something else?' she asked evenly—and found he would be the one to decide when to change the subject.

'It embarrasses you talking of your lover?' he grated toughly. 'The man you're enjoying behind his wife's back?'

'There isn't...' she flared, but saw, as Latham glowered, ready to disbelieve any denial she made, that she was wasting her breath. 'I'm not here about me!' she stated stiffly.

'No?'

'No!' she replied shortly, and, as he placed his cup down on the table beside hers, felt her right hand itch with wayward tendencies again.

'Then—let me guess—it must have something to do with your sister.'

'You know damn well it is!' she snapped—he really was asking for it.

'Do I?' he drawled. 'The last time you were here, supposedly on the same errand, you—er—forgive me for being indelicate,' he inserted, not looking in the slightest apologetic, 'you showed every sign of—wanting my body.'

That was it! In a flash she was on her feet—only to feel the firm grip of his hand on her arm pulling her down again. Clearly he was of the view that he was the one who would decide when this discussion was over. Fuming, furious, she resisted as long as she was able, but his superior strength won, and she was pulled back to the place she had just jumped up from.

Only in doing so, in Latham taking his hand from her arm, she fell awkwardly against him—and his hand accidentally brushed across her breast. 'Oh!' she gasped, frissons of electricity rocketing through her as her eyes shot to his.

Latham stared back, his aggression, like hers, dented. She felt powerless to move. His hand was still near to her breast, and she felt that she was not even breathing when, unhurriedly, as if he had liked that brief flirtation with her breast, Latham moved his hand—and cupped it over her breast.

She stared at him, the gamut of emotions rioting in her. She wanted to tell him no, but was too transfixed to move, too transfixed to speak. Gently then he began to mould her breast beneath his hand, and as she gasped, so she strove for calm.

Once more he gently moulded the full, rounded contour he held captive, and Belvia bore it as best she could. But when he teased, to find the hardened peak he had created, Belvia could take no more. Desire for him was making a nonsense of her. His warmth, the sensuousness of his touch through the thin material of her dress, were blowing her mind.

'D-Don't—do that!' she whispered croakily, and on the instant his hand stilled. 'I—I...' she mumbled, and knew that, if she was to regain her scattered senses, she had to get away from him.

Dragging her eyes from him, she stood up—and this time he did not stop her. She knew vaguely that she could not leave his apartment until she had settled things with him about Josy, but, as she moved from the room, Belvia was more concerned just then with finding some self-control than with talking to him about her sister.

Why instinct should lead her not out of his apartment but into his kitchen she had no idea, but it seemed as good as any place to try and get herself back together.

The only trouble was that Latham followed her. Oh, heavens, he had the lot, and she knew she did not stand the remotest chance of gaining a scrap of control while he was in the same room. Determinedly she turned her back on him, as though hoping that not to see his intelligent and good-looking face might help her.

It did not, for the simple reason that Latham came and stood close behind her, his breath against her hair as he murmured, 'You want me, Belvia, don't you?'

She swallowed hard. Other men had kissed her and she had remained cool. This man only had to be in the same room and she wanted him. 'I'm—I'm...confused,' she admitted shakily—and knew at that moment that the advantage was all his.

Which made it more bewildering than ever that, when her resistance to him was at its lowest, when she was his for the taking, he did not take up that advantage, but, placing his hands gently on her shoulders, he just held her in a comforting clasp.

And she no longer seemed in charge of herself, nor in charge of her voice, for she could do no other than lean back and place her head against him. She felt the solid wall of his chest at the back of her. 'Oh, Latham,' she murmured.

His answer was to turn her without haste until she was face to face with him. She looked up at him and could see none of the coldness in his expression that had been there before. 'Latham.' She whispered his name again, and leant her head against him.

His arms came round her in a gentle hold, and it was bliss. He said not a word, but just held her tenderly in his arms, and she was enraptured—and knew that there was kindness in him.

She raised her head to look at him, and gently, as his head came down, they kissed. With an arm about her, he walked with her from the kitchen and back to the sitting-room, and there for long, long moments he looked into her all-giving wide brown eyes, and gently, without haste, he kissed her again.

Feeling shy suddenly, she smiled, and he smiled back, and her heart raced faster than ever. She raised her arms and put them round him and, purely because she wanted to, because she had to, she stretched up and kissed him. It was a lovely, wonderful kiss, and, when she pulled back to smile at him again, Latham responded by kissing her, by holding her that bit more firmly—and everything in her went haywire.

She pressed close to him; he pressed back. He kissed her throat; she clung on to him, the warmth of his body through his thin shirt making her want to feel more of him—and in no time fires of wanting were burning uncontrollably in her. As his hands caressed her back, so her hands caressed him.

She wanted him to undo the zip of her dress as he had the last time, but he did not, but just held her, and kissed her, and drove her mad with her need for him when long, sensitive fingers caressed the front of her ribcage, and upwards.

There was no thought in her head to tell him, Don't do that, when once more he gently cupped one of her breasts in his hand. 'Oh, Latham,' she murmured in joy. Nor was there any thought in her head that the last time she had been in his arms he had rejected her—this time it was different, not only because he had started to make love to her gently. It was just that she knew it was different.

'Are you all right?' he breathed.

'Oh, yes,' she replied gloriously, and knew more delight when his expert fingers did go to the zip of her dress.

A moment later and the zip was undone to her waist. With sensitive fingers Latham eased her dress from her shoulders, from her arms—and that, ridiculously she felt, was when she experienced such a shyness that, as her dress started to fall from her and a vision of herself standing there in little but her lacy underwear shot through her head, she caught a fast hold of it before it could fall from her waist.

'Something wrong?' he queried softly, teasingly.

'I'm—um—a bit shy,' she mumbled.

'Shy?' he echoed, but, as he bent his head to kiss her lace-covered breast, he seemed to accept that some family trait of shyness was getting to her.

But Belvia, even as her senses were assaulted by fresh, mind-boggling sensations at the feel of his mouth on the swell of her breast, suddenly knew why she wanted him to be her first lover—and, contradictorily, why it was just not right.

'I—don't want to!' she choked, and was not surprised, after the signals she had been giving off, that Latham should straighten and stare at her in disbelief.

'You—don't want to?' he echoed, his gaze going from the agitated rise and fall of her lace-covered breast and up to her face.

'It's—not right,' she choked. She wanted him to love her, for this first time to be with a man—who loved her.

'Not right?' He stared at her incredulously.

She took a step back, making a hash of it when with nervous fingers she struggled to get her arms back into her dress. 'I—just—can't,' she said helplessly—and started to get all het up again. He had undone the wretched zip—why the devil didn't he come and help her do it up again?

Her dress was at last done up, and she dared a glance at him. Any warmth she had imagined in his eyes was gone. Nor was his tone the sweetest she had ever heard, when he grunted, 'Are you like this with him?'

'With him?'

'Your lover!' he snarled.

'Oh, go to...' she began to erupt, then remembered very belatedly that she was there on behalf of her sister, but knew on her own behalf that she was too stewed up to start a discussion about Josy now. 'Can I ring you?' she asked.

He surveyed her sardonically. 'Am I to gather from that that you aren't staying the night?'

Again she wanted to hit him, even while she still wanted him. She hated the brutal, sarcastic swine. 'Not another minute!' she snapped, and got out of there. Damn him, damn him, damn him! She had wondered what could happen to her that had not happened to her already. And now she knew!

She, stupidly, idiotically, had fallen in love with him, and he—he did not care a button for her! He had desired her, but cared so little he had not pressed her to stay. And she, idiot that she was, felt that, had he asked her with any kindness not to go—regardless of her beliefs on a mutual love when she gave herself—she might have stayed.

CHAPTER FIVE

THERE had been a hopeful notion in her head when she went to sleep that she might wake up and find that she had made a mistake, would wake to find that she was not, after all, in love with Latham Tavenner. But, from the moment Belvia opened her eyes on Monday morning, she knew just how ridiculous that hope had been. She knew, and it was a part of her, that she was heart and soul in love with him.

It was not just physical, she knew that undeniably too. It seemed to her to be a love that transcended everything, even the fact that—given that she and Latham struck physical sparks off each other—he had shown distinctly that he preferred Josy to her. In fact, he had shown that he did not care for her at all.

'How was Kate?' Josy asked when Belvia went downstairs to assist with breakfast—and caused her to do a rapid rethink, to recall that she had used Kate as an excuse for going out last night.

'Fine. Enjoying life,' Belvia answered—and was glad to have her head in the cutlery-drawer so that she need not look her sister in the eye.

'It's about time you found yourself another job,' her father complained when Belvia placed a plate of bacon and eggs in front of him.

'What brought that on?' she enquired, and received a grunt for her trouble—no doubt his weekend had not come up to expectations. Or was it that his money worries were getting to him?

Oh, grief, she fretted, for it seemed to her that while keeping Josy out of Latham's clutches, she had been a bit tardy in remembering that—for her father's sake and for the continuance of Fereday Products—she also had most particularly to keep Latham sweet.

Great! How sweet was one furious blow to the side of his face? And how about—having shown herself more than willing to make love with him—suddenly halting proceedings by telling him 'I don't want to'? Sweet? If that was keeping him sweet, she would be lucky if he gave her father so much as the time of day next time he saw him—let alone the enormous finance he was after.

'More coffee?' She was brought out of her reverie by Josy waving the coffee-pot.

'No, thanks,' she replied, and with a sinking heart remembered that, for Josy's sake, she had asked Latham if she could phone him. But while her love for him made her want some contact with him again—quite desperately did she need some contact—at the same time she was most reluctant to make that call.

Would he expect her to ring? After last night, perhaps not. Though, since she had gone to see him with the specific purpose of talking to him about Josy, perhaps yes.

The whole of Monday went by and, although Belvia was close to the phone many times, she did not pick it up to make that call.

It was the same on Tuesday too, but on Wednesday Belvia got up and told herself she was made of sterner stuff than to go to pieces on hearing the voice of the man she loved on the other end of the phone.

Even so, nine o'clock came and went and she decided she would leave it a while and give him a chance to read his morning's mail. At half-past nine, Josy was in the vicinity of the telephone and, having let her sister think that she had nothing to worry about where Latham was concerned, Belvia did not wish her to overhear her conversation.

At half-past ten Belvia decided she was utterly and totally fed up with the dithery person she had become. She had just decided that she would go out and make her call from a telephone kiosk, however, when there was a ring at the doorbell.

'I'll get it,' she volunteered, and left Josy tidying up the sitting-room.

She had no idea who might be calling, and went to answer thinking more about the phone call she had to make than about who would be standing on the other side of the door.

Which left her totally unprepared. For, when she pulled back the door, her heart very nearly leapt out of her body to see the tall, dark-haired immaculately suited, sophisticated man she loved.

'Er...' Her voice dried and colour flared in her face—she loved him more than she had thought.

Latham's grey eyes rested on her flare of colour. 'Good lord, I didn't know women still did that!'

'And I didn't know men were so ungallant as to mention it!' she found a touch of spirit to retort, and hoped with all she had that he would think her colour came from the fact that she had been half-undressed the last time they had seen each other, and not from the fact that she loved him and that to see him was such a joy. Which was why, to counteract any stray 'I love you' vibe he might have picked up, she told him aggressively, 'Josy isn't in!'

Latham coolly studied her for some seconds, her aggressiveness not lost on him either. Nor was there any smile on his face when, grittily, he replied, 'I haven't come to see your sister.'

'Oh!' Belvia exclaimed faintly, and her heart fluttered idiotically and her throat dried. 'You've—come to see me?' she asked.

'There, you see—I knew you were intelligent.'

Sarcastic swine! she fumed on a loving instant. Though she had to concede, since it was a foregone conclusion that her father would be at his office, that if it was not Josy, then it had to be her Latham had called to see.

'Er—come in,' she invited, and knew her brain was addled when, as he stepped over the threshold, Josy, whom she had just told him was out, came round the corner of the hall. Oh, grief! Even while Josy's startled not to say alarmed look registered, Belvia was glancing swiftly to Latham. Oh, dear, he had not taken too kindly to being lied to, she observed, as he favoured her with a superior look from down his lofty nose. Swiftly she turned back to her sister, who was her more immediate concern, and from somewhere she found a light-hearted tone in which to enquire, 'Would you excuse us, Josy? Um, Latham and I——'

'Of course,' Josy butted in, with such obvious relief that she did not need to hear any reason why she was being excluded. Her manners, however, were such that she stayed to greet their caller. 'Good morning, Mr Tavenner,' she bade him, and was all ready to take flight as he answered her pleasantly,

'Good morning, Josy.'

As her sister went kitchenwards, Belvia made enormous efforts to get herself more of one piece. 'Shall we go to the sitting-room?' She addressed Latham over her shoulder, knowing that so much as to glance his way until she was more in control would negate all her efforts in that department.

She was still wondering why had he called. What, if he did not want to see her sister—as he had claimed— was he doing there? Why, she was agitating as he followed her into the tastefully furnished sitting-room, did he want to see *her*?

He closed the door behind him, and she turned, looked at his dear face—and knew, as her heart renewed its fluttering, that to do so was a mistake. For he was staring directly at her, scrutinising her face, taking in her jeans and T-shirt-clad figure, her long legs and slender shape. She wanted to speak, but found her throat drier than ever, and doubted that anything at all lucid she might be able to find to say would be audible anyway.

Latham, however, chose that moment to save her the trouble. 'I thought,' he began as a cool opener, 'given the power there seems to be between us to stir each other—sexually——' He broke off as her eyes widened and pink tinged her cheeks. Trust him not to balk from straight talking!

She could have done without such straight talking, especially on such a subject. She was just not used to it. 'Go on,' she invited bravely.

'Taking that into account——' he took her up on her offer '—I decided it better that I come here for the discussion you wanted with me the other evening.'

'About Josy?' He nodded, and her heart leapt. He really was not anywhere near as black-hearted as she

would have had him painted. 'Take a seat,' she suggested,
never loving him more than at that moment when, not
waiting any longer for her to phone him, he had ob-
viated the need for her to come to his flat—where the
physical chemistry between them seemed to ignite—by
deciding instead to come to her home. 'Can I get you
coffee?'

'No, thanks,' he declined, and if he was in a hurry in
his busy day appeared to convey the opposite as, clearly
waiting for her to be seated first, he went and stood by
a well-padded couch.

Belvia opted to sit in a matching well-padded chair
and, as he sat down too and glanced over to her, she
realised that the floor was all hers and he was waiting
for her to get on with it.

She took a shaky breath. 'Josy's very shy,' she stated,
starting to feel agitated again.

'So you said.'

'Extremely shy.'

'You said that too.'

Belvia took another glance at him. He was sitting there
cool and calm and, since this was a meeting she had
wanted, manifestly waiting for her to get on with it. That
irked her and, as ever where he was concerned, she was
glad to feel nettled; it made her feel less all over the
place about him.

And suddenly she was erupting. 'I just can't believe
you're truly serious in your pursuit of her!'

'Why can't you?' he questioned, quick as a flash.

'Because—well, because...' Damn him! He *knew* why!
But he was waiting, watching and waiting. 'Because...'

'So tell me?'

'You know... The way you—um—sexually...'

'For you, you mean?' he queried, as she knew full well *he* had known full well all along.

'That's *exactly* what I mean!' she flared, her cheeks starting to colour again. Oh, devil take it, she fumed. She would get nowhere by being angry—not that Latham looked as though he would lose any sleep over that. But he was looking at her rather intently again, and she would have given anything to know what he was thinking.

If asked, she would have said he had his mind on the person under discussion—Josy. Which was why Belvia stared at him open-mouthed when bluntly, and quite out of the blue, he questioned toughly, 'Just how sexually active *have* you been in your life?'

'I—I...' she stammered, her thoughts leaping everywhere in an effort to get on to his wavelength. She was not sure what to make of his unexpected question. Was it that he had remembered the way she had blushed when she had opened the door and seen him standing there, and...? But he was waiting. She opted to give him the truth. 'I—haven't been...er...' Grief, this straight talking was nowhere near as easy for her as it was for him. 'You're the closest I've come...' she tried again—only to have her Latham Tavenner-thumping desires on the loose again.

For, clearly no more ready to believe her now than he had been before, Latham threw her a furious look and, as if unable to remain still, he was off the couch and standing by the fireplace. 'Don't give me that rot!' he barked, his chin jutting at an aggressive angle. 'I want the truth from you, woman, nothing less!' he snarled.

Damn you, she fumed inwardly, on the instant as furious as he. He would not believe her when she told him the truth, so to hell with him. She swallowed hard on her fury and, ready now to lie her head off if need be, agreed, 'Very well.' Though what her sexual activity had to do with what they were discussing, she failed to see. Who was she? Merely the——

'So, go on.' Apparently he felt he had waited long enough for her to begin speaking truthfully about anything.

'What about?'

His eyes narrowed, and she guessed from that narrow-eyed look that he suspected she was messing him about—and was not prepared to put up with too much more of it. 'About,' he clipped, 'your sister.'

Belvia hesitated. 'I'm—not sure...' she began.

'Get on with it!' he ordered, giving her an impatient look. And Belvia knew then that, if she did not soon start talking, any minute now Latham would be striding out of the room and would almost immediately renew his pursuit of Josy.

'Can—can I trust you?' Belvia asked, knowing that she had to tell him more than that her sister was extremely shy, but not wanting to tell him anything.

'More than I can trust you, I'd say!' he rapped.

'Damn you!' she erupted, and felt so het-up suddenly that she could not bear to be seated either. Since, however, he was occupying the floor-space over by the fireplace, she opted to go and stand looking out of the window. Though as she weighed up just how much she should tell him, and centred her thoughts on Josy and the dreadful time the dear love was going through, to her horror, she felt the prickle of tears in her eyes.

Appalled, she wanted to escape, to get herself under control. But she gulped down tears, and realised she could not escape—could not, because Latham had

moved and had come to stand close by, and she dared
not so much as turn to glance his way.

And then she had no need to, for Latham was right
behind her. 'You're distressed!' he exclaimed. She shook
her head to deny any such thing. But all at once she felt
his hands on her arms, turning her to face him, and never
had she heard his voice so kind, so gentle, as when, his
hands falling from her arms, he placed sensitive fingers
under her chin and tilted her head so she should look
at him as he asked, 'What is it, Belvia?'

She looked at him, looked into warm grey eyes, and
felt in that moment that she could tell him anything.
'Josy,' she choked. 'She's a rare person, a precious
person.' She was still striving for control as she added,
'She hasn't an evil thought in her head, an ill deed in
her body.'

'So?'

'So—I don't want her hurt.'

Quietly Latham studied her. 'I won't hurt her,' he
stated equally quietly.

'But you are hurting her,' Belvia told him urgently.
'Just by asking her out, you're hurting her.'

'She's that sensitive?' he questioned disbelievingly.

'It isn't just that——' She broke off—there was no
more she could add.

But Latham seemed to think that there was. 'Tell me
about it?' he requested, looking at her levelly.

Staring into his eyes, she saw nothing but encour-
agement there. But still she hesitated. 'I... I'm...'

'Afraid?' he guessed. Wordlessly she nodded. 'Don't
be,' he murmured. 'You can trust me, I promise you.'

Oh, Latham, she inwardly cried, in turmoil within
herself. Josy wanted nothing but to be left alone—yet

Belvia had a feeling that nothing would make this man
back off from what he was going after—unless he knew
of a very good reason why he should do so. She stared
into his eyes again, into his face, and saw nothing but
understanding there, a willingness to understand.

She turned from him and his hand dropped from her.
She stared unseeingly out of the window, still in turmoil,
but heard every word when Latham asked, 'Tell me why,
when other men must want to date your sister, I should
not.' A knife turned in her and added to Belvia's
torment—it hurt that Latham wanted to date Josy and
not her. 'She must have been out with other men,' he
added.

Belvia buried her own pain, but somehow then felt
strangely that she could trust him with absolutely anything. 'Only one—and he was very special to her,' she
heard her own voice answer.

'Was?' he picked up.

Belvia bit her lip. They did not come any sharper than
Latham Tavenner. 'He—died.'

'Recently?'

'Not four months ago.'

Latham was silent for a moment or two, and again
she would have given anything to know what he was
thinking. 'Why didn't your father say?' he asked, and
from that Belvia guessed that Latham would have soft-
pedalled a bit had he known. A warmth for the man she
loved washed over her and she moved from the window
to her chair, afraid this time that some of her warmth
of feeling for him might show.

Latham returned to his seat on the couch, but when
he looked at her, just sat and looked at her without saying

a word, she knew that he was silently reminding her that there was an answer outstanding.

'My father... he knows next to nothing about it,' she had to confess.

'He doesn't know your sister had someone very special in her life—and lost him?' Latham questioned, keeping any incredulity that he might feel out of his voice, but his enquiry nevertheless telling Belvia that, having got her to open up, he would insist on knowing all that there was to know—that he wanted every i dotted and every t crossed.

'Josy—didn't want him to know,' Belvia found herself telling him.

'So you kept quiet about it too?'

'Josy asked me not to say anything,' she replied—and soon had any hopes that that might be the end of his questioning dashed.

For, 'Why?' he asked.

'Why?' she repeated, and saw from his face that he knew she was playing for time—and was insisting on an answer. 'Why, because... Well, as you know...' She looked at him and saw there was no let-up in his want-to-know-everything expression. 'Well,' she set off again, 'as you know, my sister is painfully shy—always has been with strangers.'

'Yes, I know that,' he agreed quietly, and there was something in his voice which seemed to Belvia just then to be totally sensitive to what she was saying.

She looked across at him, saw the hint of an encouraging smile on his face, and loved him—and found she was going on to reveal, 'But while she has always been shy with humans, Josy has always been in her element with animals—horses in particular.'

'She owns a horse, I believe.'

Belvia nodded, warming to him for his kind tone. 'We inherited some money from our mother when we were twenty-one, eighteen months ago, and Josy bought Hetty with some of her money, and——'

'What did you do with yours?'

Belvia blinked. His question was unexpected; they had been talking about Josy. 'Oh, I threw in the job I was doing at the time and went into training for something I really wanted to do,' she replied with a smile. She saw his serious glance seem to pause a moment, then move to her curving mouth, and a flutter of emotion washed over her just at being in the same room with him. 'Er— anyhow, it was a lovely time for us both. I was doing something I enjoyed, and Josy had Hetty. We haven't room for stabling ourselves,' she went on, 'but that was no problem because there's a riding-stables a couple of miles from here and Josy arranged to have Hetty stabled there.'

'Presumably she went to see her horse every day?'

'Oh, she did. It was such a happy time for her,' Belvia replied, remembering how it had been. 'As soon as she had her chores for the day done she would be up at the stables, Saturday, Sunday, rain or shine. Over a period of time, though,' she continued, her voice starting to dip as she remembered, 'the more she went to the stables, the more she began to relax with a man who was a groom there. Then one day she confided to me about Marc...' Her voice faded, Josy's pain her pain.

'She had fallen in love?' Latham queried gently.

Belvia nodded, too full of emotion to speak. She made a coughing sound to clear her constricted throat, and was remembering it as it had been when she went on to reveal, 'It was a very big moment for her on the day she asked Father if she could invite Marc home to introduce him.'

'Your father was not too pleased with the idea.'

'How did you...?' Her voice tailed off. Good grief, where was her brain? Her father was trying to impress Latham, yet here she was within an ace of revealing what an out-and-out snob her father was! 'My father wants only what's best for Josy. For me too,' she added hastily, in her hope to make him see her father in a better light.

'But you didn't want to marry a groom,' Latham pointed out, and she wished she had not included herself in this. Neither she nor anything to do with her was why he was here.

'How did you know that Josy wanted to marry Marc?' She opted for diversionary tactics.

'It's obvious.'

She realised it probably was, and her glance slid from him. 'I suppose it is,' she agreed.

'But your father said no, that he didn't wish your sister to marry her love.'

'Josy didn't ask for either his blessing or consent.'

'Didn't she, now?'

Belvia shook her head. 'No,' she replied, and knew he wanted more, but she could not tell him more.

That was, she was certain she could not tell him more while he was seated on the couch. But when suddenly, although completely without haste, he left his seat and came and sat on the arm of her chair, her certainty became clouded by confusion. He was close, too close; his nearness was making a nonsense of her. When he bent down and gently took her hands in his, and queried softly, 'So?' Belvia had the hardest work in the world to hide from him her innermost feelings for him.

'So she married, without telling him,' she replied—and was aghast at what she had just said. 'I...'

'Your father didn't know one of his daughters got married?' Latham asked, his surprise evident.

'He—he still doesn't know,' she stammered in a rush, as, appalled by what she had revealed, she hastened to repair what she had done—for Josy's sake she had to get Latham to promise not to say a word to her father. 'Josy proved stronger and more spirited than I'd have thought when she decided to marry Marc and tell Father after the honeymoon. But...'

'Was that when Marc died, on their honeymoon?' Latham asked.

Belvia realised that, since she had said Josy had been going to tell their father after her honeymoon, it was not so very difficult to work out that a tragedy had befallen Marc before the honeymoon was over.

'Yes,' she confirmed. 'Josy told father she was going away for a few days—which stretched. I was at the wedding. Just me and another witness. I cried buckets, I was so happy for her,' she inserted, but went swiftly on, anxious, now that she had said so much, to get it all said. 'They went away to Marc's people in France, to tell them of their marriage and to honeymoon there. But only the next day Josy phoned from France to say Marc was dead.'

'You flew at once to her,' Latham stated, as if he knew it for a fact.

'That's about it. I took a few minutes out to leave a message with my father's secretary to the effect that I'd decided to take a short holiday too—and went. Josy was in shock—we flew back after the funeral.'

'And you *still* didn't tell your father what had happened?' Latham queried, his incredulity straining at the leash.

'It's the way Josy wants it,' Belvia replied, clamping her lips firmly shut on words such as: who could blame her sister after the way their father had been about Marc?

'You're reiterating that your father knows nothing of your sister's marriage?'

'I am.'

'That he has no idea that she's a widow?'

'He doesn't,' she answered, adding quickly, 'And I'd ask you to respect what I've told you. Give me your w——'

'Didn't your father notice she was in a state of shock?' Latham cut through what she was saying to question her.

'Josy's always been incapacitated by shyness.'

'Within her own family?' he asked, an eyebrow arching in surprise.

'No, of course not. But she's always been quiet, so— Well, my father's a busy man—he probably wouldn't notice if she was a little more quiet than usual, and anyhow...' Her voice tailed off, but he would not allow her to leave it there.

'Anyhow—what?' he pressed.

She shrugged. 'Anyhow, I covered for her every time she dashed from the room to howl somewhere in private.'

Momentarily she felt the grip he still had on her hands tighten. Then he abruptly let go and, getting up from the arm of her chair, he went and stood again over by the fireplace.

And it was from there that, to her astonishment, he clearly stated, 'All of which goes to show that you're a pretty wonderful sister.'

Her mouth fell open. What had brought that on? They had been talking about Josy, not her. He had made a nonsense of her again—just one compliment from him, that was all it took, and she went weak. But, for Josy's sake, she had to be strong.

That knowledge left her struggling and searching around for some comment which would for a second time take attention away from herself. 'I've heard tell that you're a pretty wonderful brother,' she found out of nowhere, with no idea just then where she'd heard it, and, her head still not together, little more idea about anything else either.

Her comment had the desired effect, however, in that Latham threw her a far from complimentary look and scowled at her, as if being reminded of his sister had brought to mind some unpleasant memory. Was he perhaps not such good friends with his sister as she had believed? she wondered.

Whatever the case, Belvia saw, as he drummed his fingers on the mantelpiece while, deep in thought, he stared hostilely at her, that his mood had undergone a sudden change.

Nor was it for the better, she discovered, when, all sign of gentleness and understanding gone, he asked harshly, 'Bearing in mind your mammoth propensity for telling lies—how much of what you've just told me should I believe?'

The swine! To get her talking—and then to turn on her! In the next moment she was on her feet, facing him, staring him straight in the eye. 'Everything I've told you about my sister is true!' she snapped. She was starting to shake inside but did not know whether it was from anger, or just from an emotional reaction to him; all she knew then was that, before he left her home, she wanted his word that he would repeat none of what she had told him. 'And,' she went on hurriedly, 'I'd like your promise that you won't say anything to my father of what I've told you.'

For an answer he favoured her with an arrogant stare. 'Is that all?' he questioned curtly.

He was annoying her again—an indulgence she could not afford. To hide her annoyance she wandered to the back of the couch when she thought she had got herself sufficiently under control to answer his question. 'As a matter of fact, no,' she replied. Raising her head, her eyes, she looked at him. God, he looked tough. 'I should also like your promise that you'll back off,' she made herself go on.

'Back off?'

Ooh, what she would not give to have another crack at him. The baiting brute, he knew damn well what she was talking about. 'Josy,' she stated succinctly. 'My sister. Will you leave her alone?' Confound it, what was this man doing to her? A moment ago she had been more or less demanding that he leave Josy alone, yet now, in less than five seconds, she was almost pleading with him to leave her alone. 'It can't be that you l-love her, can it?' she asked, and did not know, as she waited for him to answer, how she would be able to take it if he answered that he did love her sister.

But he did not answer and, even while her heart beat anxiously, Belvia began to hate him because, without

saying a word, he could—because of force of circumstances—make her go from demanding to pleading.

'Please,' she requested, and was left having to ask,
'Please tell me what you intend to do.'

Latham moved away from the fireplace, and as he
came nearer so her heart beat the faster. But the couch
was still between them when, after studying her earnest
expression for a few moments more, he began, 'I'll...'
He paused. 'Let you know.'

'Oh, please!' she cried—really, this just was not good
enough.

But he was already on his way to the door, and the
only promise she got was the, 'I'll be in touch,' which
he threw over his shoulder on his way out.

CHAPTER SIX

BELVIA spent the following hours in an agony of anguish, and that anguish was still with her when she awoke on Thursday morning. No sooner had Latham departed the day before than she had realised that, by telling him all she had about Josy, he could have her jumping through hoops! If he so desired he could make her do anything he wanted and—if she was to protect her sister from him—there was not a thing she could do about it. She was at his mercy whatever he, with his 'I'll be in touch,' decided.

She knew why she had told him so much, of course. From the love she bore him, she had felt she could trust him. That he had seemed sensitive and understanding had gone a long way towards that trust, but it was of no help to her now. And while it was unfortunately true that the love that had grown in her for him—which had come unannounced and unwanted—was of such strength that she thought that there was nothing she would not do for him, the wealth of love she had for her still-vulnerable sister meant that she would do all in her power to protect her.

Belvia got out of bed wondering when Latham would be 'in touch'. She had half expected him to ring last night, and had half jumped out of her skin when the phone had rung. But the call had not been for her but for her father, in connection with a golf tournament Fereday Products were co-sponsoring on Sunday. How,

110

when Fereday Products were next door to broke, they could co-sponsor anything, defeated her. Though, according to her father, to be *seen* to be prosperous was everything.

She pushed Latham out of her head and went downstairs, starting to hope that today she might not have to resort to lying her head off.

She had had little compunction in telling a whole string of whoppers to the man she loved, but liked less having to lie to her sister. Yet she had been totally stumped yesterday, when no sooner had he gone, Josy had sought her out and asked anxiously, 'What did he want?' The truth, that Latham was still after Josy, had had to be avoided at all costs.

'Oh, nothing too important,' she had replied, while her thoughts had gone scurrying to come up with a reason that had nothing to do with Josy, nor Latham either. 'We—er—— You know that concert thing I went to with him the other Monday,' she had pulled out of an unknown somewhere.

'Yes,' Josy had replied, giving Belvia another second to get her powers of super-invention into gear.

'Well, that night——'

'You were all right? You weren't harmed in any way?' Josy had cut in in utmost concern, giving her not only another couple of seconds but the gleam of an idea.

'No, I told you, Latham's manners were impeccable,' she had smiled. 'But during the evening I met a man called Rodney Phillips who works for Latham.' And it was here that the truth had started to stretch. 'Anyhow, Rodney Phillips asked Latham for my phone number, apparently, and it was only after he'd given it to him that his PA told him that Rodney has a terrible reputation for being rather unpleasant with women when he's had a drink or two. Latham was more or less passing our door when he felt he was morally bound to come and pass on what his PA had said, because he feels sure that Rodney Phillips might phone and ask me out.'

'That was very decent of him,' Josy had opined—and had left Belvia feeling a trifle stunned at her unexpected powers of invention, and sending a silent apology to Rodney Phillips, whom she had judged to be totally harmless.

And the phone stayed silent. Belvia went to bed on Thursday night feeling het-up and angry. She hated this waiting game, this guarding the telephone, this going out only to exercise Hetty and dashing back fearful that Latham might have phoned in her absence.

'Fancy coming to the supermarket with me?' Josy asked her just after eleven on Friday morning.

There and back, with shopping in between, the supermarket was a two-hour trip. 'Do you mind if I don't? I promised myself I'd do a wardrobe clear-out today, and if I don't soon get started I'll——'

'If you're throwing out your green two-piece, put my name on it,' Josy butted in—and Belvia could not have been better pleased. Not because her sister had taken her excuse without offence, but because this was the first time in an age that she had shown the smallest interest in clothes. Was she starting to recover? Oh, she did so hope so. It was only a small step, Belvia knew that, but it was a step in the right direction.

Josy had been gone only about fifteen minutes when the doorbell sounded, and Belvia's stomach tightened in knots. It would not be him, it could not be him, she told herself as she went to answer it. What busy man of business could afford to take time out of his schedule twice in one week for something that had nothing to do with business?

Nervously she put her hand on the door-catch, and had to take a deep and steadying breath before she opened it—and it was him. And her heart sang and danced just to see him—casually clothed, even though this was the middle of a business day.

In return Latham was eyeing her, taking in her tailored trousers with crisp shirt tucked into the waistband. What he was thinking she could not tell, for his expression told her nothing. 'Me—or Josy?' she asked, as she attempted to steady her heartbeat by reminding herself that his visit might bode nothing good for her sister.

Latham eyed her unblinkingly for a few seconds longer. Then, clearly remembering their exchange the last time she had opened the door to him, when she had said that Josy was not in and he had replied that it was not Josy he had come to see, 'You,' he clipped.

Belvia did not make the mistake of offering him coffee this time. This man, for all his casual air, meant business. She remembered how she had realised that, having handed him all the aces, so to speak, she had placed herself entirely at his mercy—and tried not to panic.

'We'll go to the sitting-room,' she stated, and led the way. He followed without saying another word, and in the sitting-room Belvia pointed to the chair she had sat in on Wednesday while she went over to the couch. They were both seated when, perhaps hoping to defer what she guessed in advance might be something not too pleasant, 'Josy really is out today,' she commented.

'Somewhere interesting?'

'Only the supermarket,' she replied, and suddenly wanted it all said and done so that she would know the worst.

As too did Latham apparently want it all said, for, his tone crisp, he asked, 'Is Josy well enough for you to leave her for a few days?'

Belvia shot him a wary look. In point of fact, while returning her affection, Josy enjoyed solitude sometimes and, if her comment about the green two-piece was anything to go by, had made a start on recovery.

But Belvia had no intention of telling him that—she had been far too open before. 'What do you have in mind?' she hedged, and found she was looking into a pair of cool grey eyes which never flinched.

'I've a country retreat in Wiltshire where I occasionally spend a weekend. I'm on my way there now, as a matter of fact.'

'Oh, yes?' she queried politely.

'I've invited some people down tomorrow, a married couple. They'll stay overnight, and,' he added, 'I'd like you to come with me, and be there too.'

For a moment, as what he said penetrated, her thoughts went haywire. The thought of spending the whole of today with him, of being with him for the whole weekend, albeit with other people as from tomorrow, sounded like absolute bliss. Suddenly, though, she crashed down back to earth. It was not as simple as that—he did not love her—and there were strings.

'Why?' she asked shortly.

Latham shrugged. 'While you may not be such a good housekeeper as your sister, I'm sure you'd be able to cope in the kitchen.'

So he wanted her to cook for him and his guests. Belvia could not see that as any problem, but—she had trusted him without thinking on Wednesday, and had regretted it ever since.

'What's this got to do with Josy?' she asked—the question which was at the basis of her knowing him.

'The decision is yours. Come with me—and your sister will not be bothered by me ever again.'

Belvia's breath caught. Surely for him to be able to state that so categorically had to mean that he was not in love with Josy, didn't it? Oh, how wonderful! Suddenly her heart was singing. Man-like, Latham had only been interested in her sister because she was unattainable, but he had no deep love for her.

Suddenly Belvia realised she was going off into orbit in her relief—and so fought hard to counteract it. Why should she go and be his skivvy? she made herself think belligerently—only to be tripped up by thoughts of not only her sister but her father also. And—oh, grief—her father would only have to hear the merest whisper of what had gone on and without question, if he knew she had refused, should Latham so request her sister the next time, he would put pressure on Josy to go.

Abruptly a stray strand of caution came to Belvia, which blotted out all other thoughts and, before she knew it, she was blurting out shortly, 'I'd have a room to myself?'

Of course she would, she realised on the next moment, and, feeling dreadfully embarrassed all at once, she wished she had stayed quiet. Though she was not at all sure about the mild-mannered smile that came to Latham's expression as he scrutinised her anxious face for a few seconds. She did not trust that mild-mannered smile.

Then she found that she had indeed worried unnecessarily, for, not missing that she had just as good as told him she would go with him, he replied, 'The property is a three-bedroom cottage.' Relief rushed in that of course she was to have her own room. But, as Latham's mild-mannered smile took on a silky edge, Belvia began to grow wary again, and was soon learning that her relief had been premature. As too had any thought that she had worried unnecessarily because, without so much as a change·in tone, Latham went on, 'Unfortunately, I've had the middle bedroom converted into two *en suite* bathrooms.'

Her throat dried, but she would not swallow and show him how this news was affecting her nerves—she would not. 'So—your cottage is now a two-bedroom cottage?' Bother his wanting every i dotted, every t crossed. Before she so much as set foot outside her home, she wanted every fact established.

'Your training in accountancy is standing you in good stead,' he murmured sardonically, and again she wanted to hit him—it did not require a calculator to subtract one from three to make it two.

'So,' she pressed doggedly on, 'where would I sleep.'

'Oh, I wouldn't dream of allowing you to sleep anywhere but in a bedroom,' he answered pleasantly, adding, 'And to save your next question—I've no intention of dossing down on the sitting-room sofa, either.'

Belvia swallowed then, despite her determination not to; she just could not help it. But she was still as dogged as ever to find out at the outset just what went on here.

'You're not suggesting for a moment, I suppose, that I share a room with your female guest while you...?' He was shaking his head long before she could finish.

'Not for a moment,' he agreed casually.

God, how she hated, loved, hated him! 'You're saying that, when your guests arrive tomorrow, I'm to sleep in the same room as you?' she insisted on knowing.

He smiled a smile of pure mockery. 'There, I *was* right,' he drawled. 'You are bright.'

Oh, how she wanted to wipe all that mockery from his face. Failing that, she threw him a cutting look that did not even dent him, and fought a panicky but losing battle within herself. She would not go, most definitely she would not go, was her first thought. Then she thought of Josy—and knew without a single doubt that if she did not go, then he would feel free to renew his pursuit of her sister.

Nerves were most definitely starting to bite when Belvia stared at him hostilely, and demanded, 'You'd expect me to sleep in your bed?'

His mouth twitched and, at the thought that he must find it amusing that she could be so hostile and yet ask such a question, she again wanted to hit him. 'If you absolutely can't resist it,' he mocked, and veritable sparks of outrage and impotent fury flashed in her eyes.

The pig! The arrant swine! The diabolical rat! He damn well knew what he could do to her! Damn him to hell. 'What about my reputation?' she erupted, that appearing to be about her only defence. Stuff his bed— she'd sleep on the floor sooner!

'Ye gods!' he exclaimed. 'She's gone old-fashioned on me!' Belvia shot out of her chair, too furious to sit. She stormed over to the window—if she went anywhere near him she would hammer his head in. She was not looking at him, but knew he was on his feet too—and a harshness had entered his tones when he grated, 'What reputation?'

She guessed she had rather walked into that. Though if he thought she was having an affair with a married man he was not taking into account that she might have something better to do with her weekend than go off somewhere with him. Not, on second thoughts, that what she wanted was of the slightest importance to him.

She turned to look at him standing by the mantelpiece and gave him a withering look, which bounced off him. 'What if I don't come and—for the want of a better word—housekeep for——?'

'Hostess,' Latham cut in coolly, and as coolly and effectively answered the question she had not finished asking by querying, 'When will your sister be back?'

Which as good as told her it was her—or Josy. 'You're bluffing!' Belvia challenged, somehow unable to believe she could have fallen in love with a man who, after all she had revealed of her sister's widowhood, could be so hard.

His answer was to stride to the door without further comment. Her bluff called, Belvia was galvanised into action and reached the door at the same time as he did. 'You win!' she gasped, with no doubt in her mind then that if she allowed Latham to go from the room he would waste no more time with her, but would relentlessly go after her sister. She stared up at him from wide brown eyes, loved him and felt defeated, but knew that it was not over yet. 'Have I your promise that, if I do share a room with you, you won't—er—come over all—er—amorous?' she asked quietly.

His answer was at first to stare down into her eyes with a look so bordering on gentleness that her heartbeat suddenly started to race. She felt he was on the point of telling her to forget the whole thing. But then suddenly something seemed to come over him, and all at once that gentle look had hardened, and then had changed again, and a look of utter wickedness was on his face when he mocked, 'What about *my* virtue?'

How she kept her hand off him then, she did not know—but she had only one more question to ask. 'If I do this—you'll leave my sister alone?'

He looked at her seriously for long, long moments, and then it was that he told her what she wanted to hear. 'You have my word,' he said quietly.

Belvia looked at him for perhaps a second longer and, the die cast, she took a shaky breath. 'I should like to leave before Josy comes back,' she decided.

His reply was to open the door. 'It shouldn't take more than a few minutes for you to throw a few things into a weekend case,' he decreed.

Without a word Belvia went past him and up the stairs to her room. Now that she accepted that she had no choice but to go, her head started to spin with un-answerable questions. Why her? He did not like her. Certainly did not love her. Her heart lightened slightly at the certainty that Latham did not love Josy either. But she had not thought the soup she had made for dinner that time had been so great that he would think of her when, despite his 'hostess' comment, he wanted a housekeeper for the weekend.

Although, on reflection, since he had only two bed-rooms, perhaps that was the reason. She got out a suitcase, and began to see that of course it was the reason. He needed someone to cook for him and his guests this weekend and, since he had nowhere to sleep a cook, on the strength of her soup she had been elected.

Any further thoughts she might have had on the subject were cut short when just then, and without so much as a knock or a by-your-leave, Latham Tavenner opened her bedroom door and walked straight in.

'I could have been changing!' she protested, and was made to weather his look that said, I've seen you half undressed before, so why the noise?

She clamped her lips together and watched astonished as he moved over to her bedroom window and glanced out. 'I thought I'd carry your case down,' he remarked, his back to her as he looked out at the view below.

Ever the gent! 'I've barely started packing yet!' she complained.

'I'll wait.' There was no end to his sauce, she fumed to herself. 'Do you do any of the garden?' he enquired conversationally.

Belvia threw him a withering look which, since he had his back to her, was wasted. 'Josy does most of it,' she replied coldly, opening drawers and throwing underwear and nightwear into her case, and darting into the bathroom for some toiletries before going smartly to the wardrobe and, concerned to get out of there before her sister returned, taking out the first things she touched. 'I'll have to write a note to Josy,' she informed the straight back of the man in her room as she snapped her case shut. 'And I'll have to make a phone call before I...'

The rest of it died in her throat when Latham left his contemplation of the garden to shoot round, and his conversational tone abruptly vanished. 'Who to?' he demanded aggressively.

'My stars!' she exploded. 'You're never the same two minutes together!'

'It's part of my charm. Who to?' he insisted.

She tossed him an irritated look and would have ignored him, but he left his place over by the window and somehow, as he came nearer, she began to feel threatened—not by him, but by what his nearness could do to her. If he touched her, laid so much as a finger on her arm... 'Oh, this is ridiculous!' she erupted. 'I merely have to ring the stables to——' Anger pure and simple caused her to break off. Since it did not look as though he intended to leave her room until she did, then he was going to overhear her conversation anyway.

To hell with him, she railed inwardly and, going over to the phone by her bed, refused to say another word to him, but dialled the number of the stables and was fortunate enough to find the person she wanted to speak to near at hand.

Once her phone call was made, she went to her writing-desk and, finding it impossible to ignore Latham, did her best anyway, only to find he was looking over her shoulder, reading everything she wrote, as she penned her note.

> 'Dear Josy,
> Kate rang—in something of a state. After-retirement blues, I think. I've said I'll go and stay with her for a few days. Rang Tracey, by the way. She'll exercise Hetty till I get back. See you some time Sunday.
> Love, Belvia.'

'Who's Kate?' Latham wanted to know.

'My God—don't tell me you missed something!' Belvia exclaimed waspishly—and knew she was very definitely going light-headed when he laughed, and she discovered that she wanted to join in. 'Kate's someone I used to work with,' she told him belligerently—anything rather than let him see that they shared the same perverse sense of humour.

Belvia left the note to her sister propped up on the hall table and went from the house, to discover that Latham had dispensed with a chauffeur's services and was driving himself that Friday.

She told herself as they drove along that she was not going to enjoy one single solitary moment of the next two days—but could not deny that her emotions were confused and all over the place just to be seated in his car with him, a whole weekend in his company stretching before her.

Latham had chosen to take the scenic route rather than the motorway, and it was nearing one when he pulled up at a pleasant-looking hotel. 'We'll lunch here,' he decided.

She loved him; it was weakening her. 'I'm not to begin my skivvying straight away, then?' she queried tartly.

'You're priceless,' he answered good-humouredly, and Belvia just did not know what to make of him. An hour earlier he'd been tough, unyielding, giving her little choice but to agree with what he wanted. Yet now, for all there had been sparse conversation between them, he was behaving most amiably and, as he came round and opened her door for her, being well-mannered to boot.

Lunch went better than she had expected, given the circumstances. It had crossed her mind that, with the two of them being scratchy with each other, she would not be able to eat a thing. But, as before, she found his manners were immaculate in company and, as she was being treated with every courtesy, it somehow rubbed off on to her, so that her own innate good manners soon surfaced. So much so that they were at the pudding stage before she realised it, the whole of the lunchtime going splendidly.

He had even made her laugh over some small incident to do with his work, but as she looked across the table at him she immediately sobered. She loved him—was that why she felt so relaxed, so utterly at one with him?

'Something wrong?' he enquired, and seemed so much at one with her too, so much in tune—instantly aware of her smallest change of mood—that her heart jerked.

She shook her head, fully aware that only a short while ago she would have replied with some tart answer. Aware too that, because of the love she had for him, she was imagining a 'togetherness' that just was not there. But even so, she loved him so much that she suddenly did not want to be the instigator of hostility. What she wanted, for just a few hours, if the gods were kind, was a pleasant time to remember. She had no idea how the rest of the weekend might go—indeed, she was doing her darnedest not to think about it but to enjoy only the present. The weekend would be over soon enough and, with Latham's word given that he would not pursue Josy, Belvia realised she would never see him after that.

She smiled at him over her coffee-cup, saw his glance at her still, and quickly veiled her eyes, lest he see anything in them of how she truly felt about him.

They were both in quiet mood, it seemed, when they went out to his car. They were later driving through a small town when, out of the blue, Latham remarked,

'Talking of supermarkets...' and, as amusement pulled the corners of her lovely mouth upwards, he glanced her way, before turning his attention to a supermarket car-park.

'This is one way to spend a Friday afternoon,' she remarked drily as, trolley in grip, they entered the mêlée.

'Is it always like this?'

'I expect so.' She laughed, loved him, and had never found supermarket-shopping so exciting. 'What do you want?'

His eyes strayed to her mouth, then slowly, as if having to drag his gaze away, up to her eyes. 'What do you suggest?'

'Me?' she queried. 'It's your shopping-trolley!'

'You're the cook,' he reminded her—but so charmingly she didn't have a chance to get uptight about her enforced role.

'I expect you've got a fridge?'

'Must have.'

She wanted to laugh again, so turned away and headed for the fresh vegetables section.

They reached Rose Cottage around five o'clock. 'This is a *cottage*?' she asked as she stood on the drive and studied the detached building, in its own grounds with not a sign of another property thereabouts.

'Like it?'

She did, given that she was starting to feel a shade nervous. She knew that in other circumstances she could be totally relaxed and happy here. 'It's lovely! How did you find it?'

'Through a friend of a friend.'

Jealousy bit, and she did not like it. Was the friend a lady-friend? She did not want to know. She turned her back on the virile look of him. 'We'd better get the shopping in.'

The inside of the cottage was everything a weekend retreat should be, she felt. A cosy, carpeted sitting-room housed a couple of padded chairs, a three-seater settee and a small table. The dining-room was much smaller, with room only for a table and four chairs, and with the kitchen leading off, of about equal size.

She helped Latham put away the food they had purchased, but was far more interested in doing a reconnoitre of the bedrooms. She had her chance when Latham decided to go outside.

Her weekend case was at the bottom of the stairs, she noted as she left the kitchen. She picked it up and, case in hand, she went up the stairs. As he had said, there were two bedrooms, separated by *en suite* bathrooms. In one of the bedrooms there were twin beds, and in the other only one—a double. Next Belvia checked the airing-cupboard. Good, there was plenty of bedlinen.

She gathered up an armful of it and set to work. First she made up the double bed. It was where she would sleep tonight. She would change the sheets for his guests in the morning. Then she went into the other bedroom. Before she started work in there, however, she took a glance out of the bedroom window, from which she could see fields and hedgerows and, just below, the side of the cottage where Latham had parked his car.

She was just about to come away from the window when a movement from within the car caught her attention. She stayed where she was, and a moment later realised that Latham was inside his car using his car phone. Only then did she realise that she had not seen a telephone inside the cottage—perfect for a weekend away from it all. Though it rather spoilt the whole idea if one then brought a phone with one, she thought. And, while hating it like blazes if Latham was on the phone to some female of his acquaintance, making social arrangements for the week to come, she pondered on whether she should telephone her sister to check that all was well.

On the basis that to do so might cause her to have to tell yet more lies, Belvia decided against it, and came away from the window to busy herself making up the two beds. Besides, as she had told Latham, Josy quite liked her own company sometimes.

Belvia was just smoothing the fresh duvet-cover on the second of the twin beds when she heard Latham enter the cottage. The following sound she heard was his footsteps as he came up the stairs—and she froze.

She straightened when, hold-all in hand, he came directly to the room she was in. Oh, thank heaven! This room must be his; she was not going to have to share the room with the double bed with him.

'I th-thought this would be your room,' she commented quickly, only her initial stammer giving away her nervousness—perhaps he had not noticed it. 'I've made up these beds and the one in the other room. I thought that——'

'Slow down,' he suggested with a calm smile.

She supposed she had rather been gabbling on like some express train in her attempt to get it all said. She smiled—had to. She still loved him. 'I thought I'd sleep in the double bed tonight—by myself,' she added quickly, in case he thought differently. 'I can change the bedding in the morning.'

Latham, his eyes holding hers, dropped his hold-all down by his feet and came over to her; wonderfully, magically, his arms came out to her, and gently, tenderly, he gathered her to him. And for a while, held gently against him, she felt at peace. Oddly, she had the most uncanny feeling, when he seemed in no hurry to let her go, that he felt some sort of comfort to have her in his arms.

But then, to show just how crazy being in love with him had made her, Latham pushed her gently away from his entirely undemanding embrace and, to send her heart soaring, dropped a breeze of a kiss on the side of her face and demanded lightly, 'What are you going to cook me for my supper, woman?'

She took a step back from him, and a side-step in the direction of the door. 'You've only just had your lunch!' she laughed.

'What's that got to do with anything?' he wanted to know—and she got out of there quickly. She felt in danger of throwing herself back into his arms.

Dinner was an uncomplicated affair of tinned soup, salmon pasta and salad, with an option of chocolate gâteau or cheese and biscuits. They both elected to have cheese.

'I'll make the coffee,' Latham volunteered.

'Why not?' Belvia replied cheerfully, and cleared some of the meal-time debris away while he attended to the coffee.

They returned to the dining-room to take their coffee, and Belvia gave herself the sternest lecture on keeping a check on her cheerfulness, her smiles, if he were not to discern that, for her, the sun rose and set with him.

'Have you had this cottage long?' she enquired, and
could have groaned aloud—he'd think she was a property
freak or something. Hadn't she asked him one time how
long he had lived in his London flat?

'Not so long,' he replied amiably, but before she could
draw another breath he was preferring to go off on a
tack of his own. 'You accused me today of having missed
something—what else have I missed about you, I
wonder?'

Belvia looked at him and felt quite weak inside about
him. Which of course called for the sternest measures.
'I shall lie if I have to,' she told him, knowing from
experience that he would not leave it there.

'I don't doubt it,' he grinned. And, as if recalling that
morning in her home when, after he had read her note
to her sister, she had said, 'Don't tell me you missed
something,' he went on to refer to her note again by
asking, 'Do I gather from your note, from your phone
call to Tracey at the stables, that you've only been riding
your sister's horse because she feels unable to do so
herself—and not, as you allowed me to believe, from
selfish motives only?'

'Hey, steady there, Mr Tavenner—go on like that and
you'll be finding out I'm not so very terrible after all,'
she warned, her insides playing havoc with her at the
warm look that came to his eyes. It was time, she felt,
to talk of something else. 'Do you ride?' she asked. 'But
of course you do.'

'Do I?'

'You wanted Josy's opinion about a horse you were
thinking of buying one time,' she reminded him, certain
now, as she had been then, that he'd had no
such intention.

'So I did,' he replied, but the devilish look in his eyes told its own story.

'And you've no doubt that *I'm* a liar?'

He gazed at her steadily for some moments before going back to the subject that had been under discussion. 'So, the moment you heard your sister's calamitous news, you took over the exercising of her horse and——' He broke off, and then, not a glimmer of a smile about him, 'When did you give up your job?' he asked suddenly, sharply.

'Three or four months ago,' she replied honestly, her thoughts too startled at this change of tack for her to think of disguising that fact, or even to wonder why she should.

'Three or four months ago!' he repeated. 'That was when your sister's husband was killed. That was the time when your sister needed you.' Belvia tried to think up a trite answer, but there wasn't one. 'For your sister, you gave up all hope of the career that you so dearly wanted,' he stated softly, 'and it wasn't from boredom with the work—as your father said.'

Oh, grief, Belvia panicked. She so wanted Latham's good opinion of her—yet if he thought for a single moment that her father had lied to him then, dealing in a world where a man's word was everything, she knew her father would not stand a chance of obtaining the huge finance he was after.

'I—er—thought it best to tell him I was bored with the job—otherwise he might have tried to persuade me to change my mind,' she invented, and, suddenly discovering that she was finding it harder and harder to lie to Latham, she sought desperately to think of something with which to change the subject. She found it in a

question that had been in and out of her head several
times that day. 'Oh, by the way, I never thought to
ask——' she made her voice casual '—but who are your
guests tomorrow?'

At once any sign of a warm light in his eyes vanished,
and she almost wished she had kept her question to
herself. Latham plainly did not care for her asking about
his guests—and that annoyed her. For heaven's sake, she
would know who they were tomorrow—she was going
to have to cook for them, *and* play hostess!

She got to her feet and went to the kitchen, carrying
her used coffee-cup and saucer with her, and conse-
quently had her back to Latham when he followed her.
She ignored him, and could see no earthly reason why
she should speak to him.

Then she found, when he moved and took the cup and
saucer out of her hand and placed them on the draining-
board, that he had moved to face her. And, what was
more, he was making her look at him when, in curt and
clipped tones, he informed her, 'My guests tomorrow
will be my sister Caroline, and her husband, Graeme
Astill.'

Graeme Astill! That name rang a clear and very unpleasant bell with her. 'Oh—I know him!' she exclaimed
jerkily, before she could stop herself—remembering
Graeme Astill for the womaniser he was. She had been
at a party, not a year ago, and he had been there—his
wife not with him—acting in a very unmarried manner.
She was faintly staggered to hear Latham say he was
married to his sister.

'You have a problem with that?' Latham demanded
grimly, the jerkiness of her exclamation not lost on him.

The fact that tomorrow she would share a bedroom with Latham, and could not see his brother-in-law keeping quiet about it at the next party he went to, made her feel uncomfortable. Some of her friends could quite easily be there too! 'And if I do?' she challenged sharply.

He looked at her grimly, a murderous light in his eyes. 'Tough,' he rapped, and, making her absolutely furious, 'You're far too free with your favours!' he added.

How she stopped herself from hitting him Belvia never knew. But, too furious to pause and analyse that remark, she somehow managed to hang on to a thread of dignity, though feeling that if she stayed near him another minute she would end up assaulting him. 'Thanks!' she snapped, and, as a red mist of rage came before her eyes, 'You're so good at making coffee—you can try your hand at washing-up!' she spat—and escaped quickly up to bed before that last thread of self-control split asunder.

CHAPTER SEVEN

BELVIA had thought she would not sleep a wink that night, but proof that she had slept was there in the fact that, having taken an age to drop off, she overslept, and was awakened by a voice in the region of the bedroom door asking sardonically, 'Do you intend to get up today?'

He sounded no more pleasant this morning than he had when, without a word of goodnight, she had left him with the washing-up. She eyed him acrimoniously—even as her heart accelerated its beat just to see him she determined that she did not like him very much that morning. 'Thanks for the tea!' she snapped sarcastically, and hated him when he favoured her with a disagreeable look and went out.

Swine, she dubbed him afresh, sat up in bed—and suddenly loved him with her whole heart. Because there reposing on the bedside table was a cup and saucer which hadn't been there when she had lain down last night. He *had* brought her a cup of tea.

What was more, when bathed and dressed she went down to the kitchen, she discovered that he had also tried his hand at washing-up because there was not a used utensil or piece of unwashed china to be seen.

At that moment the back door opened and Latham came in. 'Thanks for the tea,' she said a shade more civilly. He did not answer but, on thinking about it, there was not a lot he could say in reply. 'Have you had breakfast?' she enquired, hating herself for wanting to be pleasant to him but seeming unable to be any other way. After tomorrow she would never see him again.

'About an hour ago,' he replied and, sensing censure, Belvia gave up all half-formed thoughts of parting friends. To the devil with it, she thought crossly, and made breakfast for one.

After toast and coffee she went upstairs and stripped the bed she had used and remade it with fresh bedlinen, tidied and dusted and set about removing all traces of her own occupation from the bedroom and bathroom. Having placed all her belongings on the landing outside, all she had to do was take her weekend case and impedimenta to the other bedroom and bathroom.

She opened the door of the bedroom which Latham had used last night, though as she stood and stared in there was no sign that he had been there at all. Both beds were made, so he must have made his.

Belvia went into the room, and pulling back the duvet of the nearest bed, she saw that it had not been slept in. Fine. She slipped her nightdress beneath the pillow, took her toilet-bag into the bathroom and went to put the rest of her belongings away. In all it took her about ten minutes. But at the end of those ten minutes the fact that she would be sleeping that night in this room, she in one bed, Latham in the other, started to get to her.

In something of a hurry she left the room and went downstairs, her feelings towards her host none too sweet. He was in the kitchen having a cup of coffee, she observed, and she was then a mixture of regret that she had not offered him one when she had made her own, and of why the dickens should she? She had not asked to be brought away from the safety of her own home. Let him make his own coffee—he was big enough!

She went over to the sink just as he stood up. 'We'll go for a walk,' he announced, sounding for all the world as if he felt caged in.

What a pity! she thought scratchily, and found the sweetest pleasure in replying, 'You go for a walk! *I'm* cleaning vegetables.'

He gave her a long-suffering look—though what he thought he had to be long-suffering about she did not know—and, having apparently changed his mind about going for a walk, went and found himself something to do outside.

Good, she fumed, and missed him, and wanted him back, and wanted to go for a walk with him—but peeled potatoes and parsnips and attended to beans and broccoli, and mixed the batter for a Yorkshire pudding.

Because she had to know, and because it was just too ridiculous not to ask, she went outside to find him once the chores she had set herself were completed. Though she did not have to look very far and he, if anything, more or less found her. Because if he had been listening for the sound of her leaving the house—and possibly decamping—he could not have appeared more quickly.

'Going somewhere?' he grated.

How could she go anywhere when, until tomorrow, Josy's peace of mind was still under threat? 'Just say the word!' she offered, weathered his arrogant look, and snapped, 'What time are your guests arriving?'

'Anxious to see them?' he snarled.

'You should go back to bed and get out the other side!' she erupted, suddenly felt panicky inside, and wished she had not mentioned that word 'bed'. 'Look here,

Tavenner,' she went on crossly, 'if I'm to be cook, then I need to know what time you need feeding.'

He surveyed her angry, mutinous expression with cool detachment for some seconds. 'We'll eat this evening,' he then announced, and, as she turned about, 'For now I'll make do with a sandwich.'

What did your last servant die of? she fumed inwardly as she did an about-turn and went back inside the cottage—and then wondered, how could she? How could she think and behave like that when she loved him so much?

She could, she realised only a minute later as she got out the makings of a sandwich, because while she might love him, he did not love her. And that, without him knowing it, was painful to bear. She wanted only to store up memories, happy memories of this short time with him. But there was little chance of that. Tomorrow it would be all over and their paths would never cross again, and while she wanted only to be loving and giving to him, she could not be, because whatever happened he must never know of her love for·him.

'My sister will be here around three,' Latham announced while he ate his sandwich.

He sounded affable. 'Isn't your brother-in-law coming after all?' she asked.

His affability was an illusion. 'Does that worry you?' he snarled.

Belvia stared at him. 'God, somebody should have sorted you out when you were a child!' she flared.

'Fancy trying it?' he rapped, his jaw jutting at an aggressive angle.

'I haven't got that long!' she hissed—and suddenly, against all odds, while they were glaring angrily at each other, as his lips started to twitch, so hers did the same, and all at once they both burst out laughing. But she did not need to see him laughing and amused: their sense of humour melded as one, and... Oh, grief, she thought as he stopped and stared at her, and all she could think of to do was to order him to clear off. And, as if he was more or less thinking something of the same—he went.

Graeme Astill did arrive with his wife, but Belvia did not like him any better on meeting him for a second time than she had on the first. But good manners prevailed. She took an instant liking to Latham's sister who, in her opinion, was much too good for her husband.

'I wasn't sure what we were doing for a meal this evening.' Caroline, a tall blonde of about twenty-eight, smiled as she went into the kitchen with Belvia. 'If we're going out, fine, but if not, I've brought an apple pie— a favourite of Latham's—as my contribution.'

Belvia could have stayed listening to Caroline talk of her brother's likes and dislikes for the rest of the afternoon, but Caroline had nothing to add, and she realised that to ask anything would only show an interest in him which she would rather no one knew about. Though what did either of the Astills think she was doing there with him that weekend if she was not interested in him? Sharing a bedroom with him... Belvia blanked her mind off, and was glad that it was Latham who showed his sister and brother-in-law to their room.

Jealousy then started to nip when, with neither Caroline nor Graeme raising so much as half an eyebrow to see her there, she began to wonder if Latham was forever bringing some female away for a weekend in the country. Again she blanked her mind off, deciding that she would much rather not know.

It niggled away at her, however, and when Latham left his sister and brother-in-law upstairs and came out to the kitchen words she had not meant to say spilled from her tongue as if of their own volition. 'I expect you bring all your lady-friends here?' she questioned, and was instantly appalled, not only at her question but at the tart way she had asked it. And, even as she saw Latham halt, an alert look coming to his eyes followed by long moments of speculation, so she was searching frantically for something to add which would show that she was not the least bit interested.

He gazed at her intently, but replied tautly, 'If it worries you, apart from Caroline, you are the only female I've invited here.'

At once her jealous soul was eased. 'It doesn't worry me in the slightest!' she scorned, and, so that he should know the subject was done with, and not after all worth a mention, added, 'Caroline kindly brought an apple pie, so I won't have to bother making a pudding for afters.' He did not care a light. Since, however, he had brought her there for the sole purpose of cooking for his guests, she trotted out sarcastically, 'That is, unless you insist on my making something.'

He gave her a venomous look and she guessed he was finding her tedious. And that suited her fine. Though she began to wonder just what in creation went on in his head when, as afternoon gave way to early evening, he seemed to grow quieter and quieter.

Was it her imagination, or was he brooding about something? Was it just that, because of her love for him, she was over-sensitive where he was concerned? Was she,

in her love for him, her unrequited love for him, picking
up vibes which simply were not there?

She did not think so, but as she and Caroline served
dinner she watched him. He, she realised with something of a jolt as her glance caught his several times,
was watching her!

Heavens above, she was getting paranoid, she realised,
and determined as the fish starter gave way to sorbet,
which was followed by the main course, that she would
buck her ideas up. Since she had nothing she wished to
discuss with Latham, and had no wish whatever to
engage Graeme Astill in conversation, she was left
chatting with Caroline. Which, she discovered, was not
the smallest hardship. As she liked Caroline, so Caroline
seemed to like her.

Latham, as host, started the ball rolling, however, by
acquainting his sister with the fact that, like herself,
Belvia rode most days. He dropped out of the conversation while she and Belvia discussed the various merits
of their mounts. From there, although there was no connection, they seemed to slip naturally into a conversation on the latest fashions and, as the conversation
changed again and Latham entered it briefly, their chat
moved on and Belvia discovered that Caroline was quite
a good golfer.

'Do you play?' Caroline asked.

Belvia shook her head. 'Afraid not,' she smiled, but
was able to converse for a few more minutes on the golf
tournament her father was co-sponsoring the next day,
and then hear how Caroline had played that particular
course and thought it a good one.

Then she and Caroline cleared the used dishes away
and brought in the apple pie, which was delicious, and
Belvia said so.

'A small thing after that lovely meal you put together!' Caroline exclaimed. 'Did you bring everything with you, or did you buy locally?'

'Belvia and I raided a supermarket on the way down yesterday,' Latham cut in, and while Belvia's heart fluttered at how close his words seemed to make them—not that he meant it to be taken that way, of course—his sister looked at him in some astoundment.

'*You*—in a supermarket!' she exclaimed.

'Given a couple of cracked ankles from the occasional wayward trolley, I quite enjoyed the experience,' he replied, and Belvia so hoped he was speaking the truth, because she had loved it.

They adjourned to the sitting-room for coffee, where she was pleased to notice that Latham's brooding look had gone. Pleased, too, that she somehow found she was seated next to him on the settee, Caroline and Graeme in the two chairs at either side of the settee. Belvia owned to feeling all over the place to have Latham this near but, since she did not have to look at him unless she was speaking directly to him, she knew he would not discern any of what she was feeling.

Conversation over coffee was fairly general, but when after a while Latham got to his feet and said that he thought, in the circumstance of the two females having fed them, that the two males should do the washing-up, she thought it a brilliant idea. With luck, and remembering the mountain of washing-up out there, she might be fast asleep by the time Latham came up to share the bedroom.

'If no one minds, I think I'll go to bed,' she said as casually as she could. 'This country air...'

'I think I'll go up too,' Caroline chimed in, and Belvia could have hugged her.

'How kind!' her husband muttered—and Belvia realised that he was not too thrilled to be roped in to help with the dish-washing. But she was not concerned with his problems just then. In her view her problems were much more important than Latham's brother-in-law's—and he was a man she just could not take to.

'Night!' she murmured generally, and without so much as a flick of a glance to Latham she headed for the stairs—Caroline following.

They parted at the top of the stairs where Belvia, seemingly still casual, ambled to the room she would share with Latham. Once inside, however, the door closed to the outside world, she tore around—cleaning her teeth, taking the quickest shower on record and donning her nightdress.

Well within fifteen minutes, she would have sworn, she was in bed and ready to snick off the bedside light. She listened, but could hear no movement on or near the stairs. Good. Latham was still on kitchen fatigue and, if this morning was anything to go by, he liked to finish any job he started, and would use more time in putting all the saucepans and dishes away.

She put out the light, pulled the covers up way past her ears and tried desperately hard to fall asleep. She wanted to be sound asleep when Latham came up. She wanted to sleep solidly through the night and not to wake until Latham had left his bed in the morning.

But she could not fall asleep. What seemed like an hour later she opened her eyes, and found the room flooded with moonlight. Oh, heck—in her rush she had forgotten to close the curtains.

Belvia was on the point of getting out of bed to remedy that error when she heard a footfall on the stairs, and she stiffened and stayed still—she was not going anywhere.

By her calculations there were two pairs of feet coming up the stairs. She pulled the duvet closer around her ears and closed her eyes fast, while at the same time she aimed for rhythmic breathing.

Her rhythmic breathing fractured slightly when she heard the bedroom door open, and heard Latham come quietly into the room. He did not put on the light, and she concentrated hard on her breathing. Time seemed to crawl along agonisingly slowly for the next ten or twenty minutes as she lay listening to sounds that told her that Latham was in the habit of showering last thing at night too.

Then she heard the bathroom door close, heard Latham come and, it seemed, stand by the side of her bed—she was not going to open her eyes to find out. She was tense, and had the devil's own work to keep her breathing regular, and still could not relax when she heard the sound of the other bed taking his weight.

Annoyingly, and in no time flat, she heard the rhythm of his regular breathing. A moment later, though, and she knew that she should be glad that he had gone out like a light. Because it was not him she was afraid of, but herself. Had he touched her, given her so much as a peck on the cheek, she was so aware of him that she doubted she would have been able to hold back from wanting more. She loved him, was in love with him, and wanted, oh, so badly to be held in his arms.

For a further age she lay there listening to his even-paced breathing, loving him with all her heart, yet knowing that in less than twenty-four hours it would be all over, that she would never see him again. The thought of never seeing him again was suddenly so dreadful that she did not know how she could take it.

How long she lay awake being torn apart by thoughts of never seeing Latham again, Belvia never knew. But eventually a welcome sleep came to give her rest.

Though it seemed to her that one minute she was ready to break her heart over Latham—and the next the bedside lamp was on and he was sitting on her bed bending over her, his hands on her upper arms as he called her name.

'Belvia, you're dreaming, wake up,' he was saying.

'What...?' She opened her eyes, took a shocked breath. 'What...?' she gasped again, looking up into his concerned face as she tried to take in where they were and tried to get a grasp on reality.

'You were creating murder in your sleep,' he explained gently. 'Don't be alarmed, you're all right.'

'Oh, Latham!' she sighed, struggling to sit up. 'Was I shouting?'

'So you do it often?' he asked, a hint of teasing humour in his voice.

'Sometimes,' she smiled. 'When I'm disturbed about something, usually—school exams, that sort of thing.'

'You're disturbed now, tonight?' he enquired, his amusement fading.

But she wanted his amusement back—she did not want to part with him on bad terms. 'Don't be cross,' she pleaded, and could no more help it than fly: not wanting to see his eyes grow cold, she leaned forward and rested her head on his chest.

She felt him go rigid, knew that he was going to push her away, but wanted just a few more moments. Then, his voice more of a growl than anything, he grated, 'Damn it, Belvia—what do you think I'm made of?' and, as if he could not stop himself, his hands came to her arms again.

But instead of pushing her away, as she had been sure was in his mind, his grip on her arms became firmer. She pulled her head back and looked into his eyes. They were not cold, but warm.

Gently, their lips met. 'Oh, Latham,' she sighed.

'You're awake?' he growled. 'Am *I* the one who's dreaming?'

She loved him; she almost told him so. 'Kiss me,' she whispered, and he did, gathering her up in his arms, and it was beautiful. She moved closer to him.

She felt his mouth gentle on hers, then, as the pressure increased, her lips parted, and Latham pulled her closer to him. 'My dear,' he breathed, and she was in a transport of wonder that his endearment for her sounded so natural on his lips.

He kissed her again, gathering her yet closer to him, and as her arms went around him she suddenly became aware that his body was naked. 'Latham!' she gasped, vaguely realising that he must have shot out of bed without thought on hearing her yelling in her sleep.

'Belvia,' he murmured.

Oh, how she loved him; she could feel his body-heat through the thinness of her nightie, and it was, oh, so wonderful to be this close to him. She kissed him, was kissed in return, and adored him when he traced tender kisses down her throat, felt her heart pound when his hands caressed her back, and felt a fierce fire of need ignite in her when gently his fingers caressed their way to her breasts. With each swollen globe captive in his hold, she had not the smallest protest to make, but wanted to cry out his name again and again. Love me, she wanted to cry, and loved him.

Again they kissed, his hands caressing to her waist, and she was on fire for him. She pressed herself to him, and wanted to be closer still, and sighed with utter content when he pushed the duvet on to the floor and, reaching for her, lay down with her, their closeness assured because the width of the bed was meant only for one.

She moved herself joyously to him, heard him groan with desire, and felt only the merest hint of shyness when, finding that her nightdress had ridden up, he took hold of the hem. 'Do you really need this?' he breathed.

'N-No,' she replied jerkily, and kept close into him so that he should not see her body when, in next to no time, they were both kneeling on the bed while he divested her of her only piece of clothing and her nightdress joined the duvet on the floor. 'C-can you...? Would you—p-put the light out?' she asked into his shoulder.

'You're—embarrassed by your body?' he questioned into her ear, a most wonderful teasing note there in his voice, holding her close against him as he reached for the light switch.

She nodded. Then corrected, 'Not embarrassed, exactly. Shy, I think.'

'Shy?'

She wanted to tell him that she had never been naked with a man before—but she knew he would not believe her, and she was afraid that it would change his mood and he would take this wonderful time away from her. So she kissed him, and pressed her naked breasts against him, and heard him groan again—and knew that he had forgotten that he had asked a question.

Gently then he eased her body from him, and in the glow of the full moon his gaze embraced her. 'Your face is beautiful—and so is your body,' he murmured and, as if to salute her beauty, he placed a gentle kiss on her mouth—and bent his head to kiss each throbbing, hardened crown of her breasts. 'My darling,' he breathed, and she was enraptured.

Tenderly he laid her down on the mattress and leaned over her, tracing wonderful, mind-bending kisses on her mouth, her breasts, her belly and her thighs.

'Oh, Latham, darling,' she breathed shyly, 'I want you so much.'

'Sweet love,' he breathed, his voice thick in his throat, and gently eased his body over hers.

Belvia put her arms around him and held him to her tightly, her mouth dry at the feel of his all-maleness against her skin, a hint of panic whispering through her aching need for him.

'Oh, now, please,' she begged on a moment of courage.

'Soon, my dear,' he promised, and moved her, stroked her thighs and kissed her. Her body seemed to answer all the signals, for, as a few more minutes passed, the time seemed to be just right when Latham kissed her and placed himself where it seemed so right to her that he should be.

'Latham!' She called his name, and it was as if hearing his name on her lips was what he needed to hear, for, a moment later, he joined her to start the ultimate part of their lovemaking. But as he moved to her, she moved to him—and felt pain, which she had been too needful of him to think of. And, 'No!' she cried—and he stilled. In the next instant, so rapidly that she could not so quickly take it in, Latham had jerked from her as if shot, and was sitting stunned, staring at her in traumatised disbelief.

'You're—a virgin!' he croaked, and shook his head as if still not believing it.

With panicking hands she reached out and caught hold of his arms. He couldn't go away from her, not now. I love you, I love you, she wanted to tell him. 'Please, please don't be angry with me,' she pleaded. 'I did try to tell you before, only...'

'Only I wouldn't listen,' he answered and, seeming to make great strides to cope with his shock, went on, 'Hell's teeth, I'm not angry with you, my love—but myself. Oh, God,' he groaned, 'I must have terrified you!'

'No, you haven't,' she denied, ready then to deny she had ever known so much as a moment's panic.

'I should have guessed, should have seen. Your shyness, your...'

It was then that Belvia began to see just how sensitive the man she was in love with was. And she leaned forward and kissed him, cutting off his words, hoping to make him see that he had nothing to hate himself for.

'I'm sorry I said no,' she whispered, putting her arms around him, holding him close. 'I didn't mean, no, I didn't want to,' she hurriedly went on to explain. 'I think it was more—I hadn't realised there would be pain. I mean, I suppose I must have known, but...' Oh, heck, she was getting herself so tangled up in knots. She just left her explanation hanging there, and said instead, 'Please make love to me.' And again she kissed him, and while she kissed him her hands caressed his back. She pressed her breasts against him, heard a desperate kind of sound and took her mouth from his to kiss his chest, and moulded herself against him.

And at last, 'Dear love,' he breathed. 'You're sure this is right for you?'

'Oh, Latham, my darling,' she cried. 'I've never been more sure about anything. I need you, I want you so badly.' She kissed him again, and against his mouth she begged, 'Please, Latham.' And she felt him respond, his arms coming around her as he took over.

This time, though, in his awareness of her virginity, Latham put a rein on his passion. She was aware of it in the slow, delicate way he brought her to new heights, teasing her breasts to wanting peaks, caressing those swollen globes with his mouth, his tongue, gently, tenderly stroking her belly, her thighs.

'Oh, Latham,' she sighed, having no idea that she could feel like this, hoping with all she had that it was the same for him. She stroked his body too.

And at last, tenderly, gently, Latham returned to her, and this time she did not cry out. For, with a wealth of consideration for the pain he must cause her, Latham moved with her in restrained passion. Moved and checked and moved, and stayed with her until he had made her totally his.

Later Latham cradled her in his arms to sleep and Belvia just could not get over it. He was wonderful—kind, gentle and overwhelmingly sensitive. She lay for some while with her eyes closed, sleep starting to tiptoe in. She felt Latham place a light kiss on her hair, and knew contentment and nothing more, until she opened her eyes again and discovered that it was daylight.

Contentment had caused her to have her best night's sleep—or what had been left of the night—since she had first met Latham. Her mental anguish seemed to have flown, for surely no man could be so gentle, so considerate, so tenderly loving if he did not feel some kind of regard for her?

She stirred in her bed and knew that, at some time while she slept, Latham must have gone to sleep in the other bed. She smiled a loving smile. Poor darling, he had waited until she had gone to sleep but must have been cramped beyond enduring while he waited for sleep to claim her.

Simply because she had to look at him she eased herself over to face the other bed and, feeling dreadfully shy suddenly—he could be awake too—she had to take another second or two before she could look across the yard or so of carpet that separated the two beds. She raised her eyes—but the other bed was empty.

For about a minute more she lay there, realising that he must be an early riser and, seeing that she was still sound asleep, must have moved especially quietly so as not to wake her. A smile touched her mouth again at his thoughtfulness. But all at once she was realising that when she went downstairs she was going to have to greet him in front of his sister and her husband.

That thought prompted her into speedy action to get bathed and dressed. While she did not doubt that Latham was sophisticated enough for him to greet her without any outward show of the closeness they had shared, she recalled her latent inclination to blush when he was around—and that was before they had lain naked with each other. By that scale of reckoning, the least she could expect was that she would go a brilliant crimson the next time she saw him.

Her hope, as she hurried down the stairs to greet Latham in private, was doomed the moment she reached the kitchen. 'I'm just making coffee—fancy one?' Caroline Astill asked her with the cheeriest of smiles.

'Love one,' Belvia responded, unable to see any sign of Latham as she busied herself getting a couple of cups and saucers out of a cupboard. And, not asking the question she wanted to ask—did Caroline know where Latham was?—she instead queried casually, 'Graeme not down yet?'

'He's gone,' Caroline informed her, something in her voice alerting Belvia to the fact that he was not merely out walking.

'Gone—where?' she enquired carefully.

'I don't know,' Caroline replied, but added, almost to herself, and as though it was a matter of some great relief, 'And I've only just realised I don't really care.'

'You—don't care?'

'I did, very much. To start with I was so much in love with him that I put up with his inconstant love.'

'Oh,' Belvia murmured. Poor Caroline. It sounded as if she knew of her husband's affairs with other women.

'Oh, indeed,' Caroline commented and, bringing two cups of coffee over to the kitchen table, she sat down and, as Belvia followed suit continued, 'Up until this morning, when I came down and saw him fall unconscious to the floor, I'd thought I was still in love with him, but——' She broke off when she observed Belvia's amazed expression.

'Graeme was unconscious? He'd been drinking...?'

Caroline shook her head. 'Latham flattened him!'

'Latham did?' Belvia was astounded. 'He hit him?'

'Knocked him clean out,' Caroline answered, and confided, 'He'd been asking for it for years, and it was beautiful to see—which is how I suddenly knew that the love I'd had for him all these years was dead. That he was a habit, and that I no longer needed him.'

There did not seem any appropriate remark to make to that, and as all that Caroline had said started to settle in her mind, so Belvia more urgently than ever wanted to know where Latham was. Had he been very upset? Must have been, she supposed. You could not knock someone out stone-cold without being furious about something. Oh, poor darling Latham. He had probably hit him from anger at the way he treated his sister. She recalled then that, while observing such courtesies as having him for a house-guest demanded, Latham had not been over-affable with him yesterday.

'Is Latham out walking?' she asked, realising that he could well have gone for a walk to cool down after flooring his brother-in-law. She was left gaping at Caroline's reply.

'He's gone back to London,' she informed her, and, catching Belvia's open-mouthed look, 'I'm sorry, didn't he say?'

'I—um—overslept.' Belvia's pride came to her aid. Her hopes, her dreams, might be fracturing about her, but she was the only one who was going to know it. 'I expect he would have said had I not been such a sleepy-head.'

'He said something about having some business to attend to. It must have been important business too——' Caroline smiled '—or he'd never have gone.' Belvia smiled back to show that it did not hurt and, seeing her smile, Caroline tacked on, 'He barely waited to blow on his knuckles after decking Graeme, then he was off.'

'That's the way it is in business,' Belvia replied and, borrowing some of Caroline's cheerfulness, she got up from the table, consulting her watch without seeing the dial. 'I suppose I'd better do something about getting back to London myself.'

'I'm returning to London myself shortly—I'll give you a lift, if you like,' Caroline offered in a friendly way.

'Didn't Graeme take the car?' Belvia paused to ask.

'It's my car, and I have the keys. With luck we might see him hitching it if we hurry. We'll give him a toot,' she added with happy maliciousness.

Belvia had to smile—but up in the room she had shared with Latham, she felt more like breaking her heart. Oh, how could she have been so unutterably foolish? The realisation that there had been nothing special for him in their lovemaking last night, nothing special at all— and that she was no more to him than some cheap, one-night fling—was crucifying.

It did not take her long to gather her belongings and to pack them, but she was so churned up inside that her hands were shaking as she fastened the catches on her case, and she just had to take a few minutes more in trying to calm herself.

Latham had been so wonderful, so sensitive with her last night, she could not help recalling, and then found that tears were streaming down her face. Oh, damn him, damn him to hell. No one had the right to make anyone feel the way she was feeling now.

Belvia dried her eyes and checked that there was no sign of her tears, then took her case downstairs. She left Caroline to lock up and did not know if she was glad or sorry that Caroline, after her initial confidence, was fairly silent on the journey back to London. She, too, plainly had a lot on her mind.

With too much time to think, Belvia tried to concentrate her thoughts during the journey on anything but Latham. But again and again he was there in her head. She recalled, painfully, how it had not been her he was interested in at all anyway, but Josy. He had done the gentlemanly thing and backed off when she had explained about her sister's recent bereavement—though it was she who'd had to pay the price.

Belvia quickly cancelled that last thought. She had no idea why he had taken her in exchange for her sister, so to speak—and she certainly was not going to ring him up and ask him. But she had no reason to complain. He had wanted a cook, and she had cooked. But it was she who had wanted him to make love to her, and he had. They had made beautiful love, but not before—at his first knowledge that she was a virgin—he had broken from her. She had urged him to stay—she had been a more than willing partner.

Caroline dropped her off at her home, apologising for not being very good company. 'It's just dawning on me that I've no one to please but myself—I think I'm going to enjoy it,' she grinned, and Belvia saw so much of Latham in his sister's grin that she could barely speak.

'Have fun!' she smiled, added her thanks for the lift and an invitation to come in for coffee and, when Caroline suggested another time, went indoors, to find Josy looking more alive than she had for a long time.

'How's Kate?' Josy asked, before Belvia could ask if anything had happened to put that light of interest in her sister's eyes.

'K——?' Belvia bucked her ideas up to remember that she had used Kate as an excuse for being away for the weekend. She evaded another outright lie. 'Anything happening here I should know about?' she enquired.

'Several things, actually,' Josy replied. 'Er—shall I make some coffee while you take your case upstairs?'

Belvia went upstairs, washed her hands and ran a comb through her hair, and caught a defeated look in the wide brown eyes that looked back at her. Since she and Josy were often so attuned to each other's smallest upset, she knew that she was going to have to guard with all she had against Josy seeing how emotionally shattered she felt.

She put her own haunted feelings to the back of her mind and returned downstairs to find that Josy had brought a tray of coffee into the sitting-room. 'So,' she encouraged, recollecting that Josy had said several things had happened, 'what happened first?'

Josy carefully poured her a cup of coffee and passed it over. 'Well, to begin with, I've been having quite a lot of private battles with myself just lately, in connection with Hetty.'

'Hetty?'

'Mm,' Josy confirmed. 'It seemed to me that I just wasn't being fair expecting you to exercise her for me the whole time.'

'Oh, love, I don't mind,' Belvia exclaimed at once.

'I know you don't—you've been marvellous. Anyhow, that hasn't stopped me from being unhappy about not exercising her myself. Anyway, I was feeling doubly guilty on Friday when I read your note and knew you'd had to consider me and Hetty before you could go to stay with Kate for the weekend.'

'Go on,' Belvia urged quickly, not needing to add guilt for telling lies to the rest of her unhappiness.

'Well,' Josy continued, 'it bothered me the whole of Friday, but I did nothing about it. I don't know now if I actually would have done anything about it if...' Her voice tailed off, and Belvia looked at her with renewed interest, sensing that something pretty gigantic had taken place in her absence.

'If?' she prompted.

'If Marc's cousin had not called in.'

'Marc's cousin—from France?'

'You've never met him. I only met him the one time myself—the day Marc and I arrived in France. He wasn't at Marc's funeral, but he's in England on some business or other,' Josy explained. 'Anyhow, I gave him coffee, and somehow, probably because Marc and I met at a stables, we seemed to naturally get round to talking about horses. Somehow, too, he began to tell me how he had a couple of mounts but how, with him being away so much, he needed someone reliable to look after them.' She took a hard swallow, and then said, 'Suddenly, as we were speaking, he all at once stopped, and then said, "I don't suppose you'd be interested in the job?" going on to tell me that he thought it might be a shade too quiet for me because he lived in an isolated spot with not too many people around.'

'You didn't say yes?' Belvia stared at her in disbelief.

'No. I said no straight away. But, since he had offered me the job, I felt that a straight no was a bit blunt, so I qualified it by telling him that I hadn't had anything to do with horses since Marc died—and he just looked at me and said, "Don't you think that you should," and talked quietly to me for quite some while—with the end result being that he wanted to see where Marc worked, and...'

'You've been up to the stables!'

'And ridden Hetty,' Josy replied to her amazement. 'And...' She got up out of her chair and seemed the same nervous Josy she had been before Belvia went away as she went over to the window and straightened two folds in the curtains before she went on. 'And before he left he asked me to consider most carefully taking on the job, to consider going to France, be it only for six months.'

'And—you have?' Belvia queried, trying to keep her astonishment hidden. This had to be Josy's decision. She must not attempt to influence her in any way. While it seemed to her, bearing in mind Josy's shy temperament, to be too tremendous a step for her to take, Belvia recalled how Josy seemed to have a penchant for occasionally surprising her and doing something entirely out of character. Look at how, when Belvia would have said the odds were more for her remaining forever a spinster, she had taken that other tremendous step and had got married.

'I'm—still thinking about it,' Josy confessed. 'But—what about Father?'

'What about him?'

'He'll hit the roof if I suggest I won't be here to housekeep for him.'

'Let him pay for a housekeeper. If he can afford to part-sponsor a golf tournament, he can afford that expense.'

'Oh, Bel, I'm so glad you're back,' Josy cried, as if Belvia had killed off some of her dragons, and then, her attention arrested by something the other side of the window, her tone quickened. 'If I did go to France for a while, though, I'd have no need to worry about Latham Tavenner, would I?' she exclaimed.

Belvia's breath caught at just the sound of his name—oh, how she wished that she could hate him. 'You don't have to worry about him any more,' she assured her quietly, and, not wanting Josy to be upset ever again, she told her that which she knew to be fact. 'I promise you, Jo, you'll never see him again.'

It was she who was the more upset of the two this time, however, because, to show just how very much she had got that wrong, Josy replied, 'I will. He's just pulled up on the drive!'

For all of ten seconds Belvia went through the gamut of emotions, so that she was incapable of coherent thinking. Then, even while her brain-patterns were all over the place, she started to grow angry. How dared he come here and badger Josy? How dared he, after...

Suddenly she caught her sister's worried look on her. 'I'll deal with him,' she stated, wanting to run a mile and crown him, all at the same time. 'How about you go into the kitchen and see about making Father's favourite pudding? It might sweeten him up if you decide you have anything you want to tell him.'

Josy did not hang about but, expertly scooping up cups and saucers on to the tray as she went, carried the tray out from the sitting-room and, as the doorbell sounded, went kitchenwards.

Belvia waited until her sister was clear of the hallway, then went to the front door. But, with her legs suddenly feeling like so much jelly, she had to lean against the stout oak door for quite some seconds. Then, impatiently, the doorbell sounded again—and Belvia, striving all the time for control, put her hand to the handle. For her own sake, for the sake of her pride—and he had left her with little enough of that—she had to be strong. He might have taken her to bed, but it was Josy he was after.

CHAPTER EIGHT

BELVIA kept her eyes lowered as she pulled back the front door but, as her gaze travelled up the long length of him, she at last had to look at him. And, as she had known she would, she blushed a furious crimson.

'My——' he began, his eyes on her face, her colour.

But she did not need any sarcastic comments from him—even if his expression did not seem to be particularly sarcastic—and from somewhere she found the acid she needed to snap tartly, 'I thought you promised to keep away from my sister!'

'You don't seriously still believe——' He broke off, seemed oddly at a loss for words, but then took what seemed to her to be a long breath, as though groping for self-control—though what he needed self-control for, she failed to see. But it appeared he had the control he needed, for his voice was even, stern almost, when he continued, 'It seems I've more explaining to do than I realised—are you going to let me come in?'

Oh, why did he have to come here? She wanted to see him, of course she did, but all she had been to him was a one-night indulgence and that did not need *any* explaining!

'Come in—if you must.' She denied her fast-beating heart even as she hated herself for her weakness. Any explaining he wanted to do could be done in two minutes on the doorstep, surely?

Having been weak enough to accede to his request, however, she turned about, leaving him to follow her into the sitting-room. Once there, though, she was un-decided whether to sit down as her shaky limbs required or, since this could not possibly take very long, remain standing.

The matter was settled for her when Latham closed the sitting-room door and went over to the couch and waited, clearly asking her permission to be seated. By that time she was afraid to speak in case she gave away, by word or look, a hint of how she felt about him.

She went over to one of the easy chairs and, by taking possession of it, let her action speak for her. Latham followed suit and, seated on the couch, turned to face her. Oh, Lord, how dear he was to her!

She lowered her eyes, studied his shoes without really seeing them—but suddenly started to grow angry. Who the devil did he think he was that he could be the way he had been with her last night and then, without so much as a word, troll off this morning when business beckoned—and then come calling at her home, as casual as you like? Dammit, what the devil did he think *she* was!

'I'm surprised you expected to find me here!' she snapped tartly, raising her eyes to give him the full ben-efit of her hostility.

'I knew you'd be here,' he replied calmly, bearing her hostility very well.

'You knew!' She added lying to his list of crimes. 'How could you know? You left me stranded at . . .' Her voice tailed off. Oh, what a fool she was—she had not meant to refer to that wonderful, sublime time in Wiltshire.

'It wasn't my intention to leave you stranded,' Latham assured her, and when she stared at him, not ready to believe a word of it, went on, 'I went back to Rose Cottage for you, only——'

'You've been back to Rose Cottage!'

'Of course I have!' he confirmed straight away. 'Leave aside my feelings when I got there and found the place locked up.' *He* had feelings! Before her startled thoughts could sort themselves out, though, he was going on. 'The obvious thing to do was to ring Caroline to enquire if she'd seen anything of you.'

'She told you she'd given me a lift.'

He nodded, and added with bone-melting gentleness, 'I wish you had waited.'

Oh, no, please don't, the weakness in her for him implored, 'You know, somehow I just knew that I'd end up being the one in the wrong!' Her mouth overrode her weakness.

'Oh, love——' he smiled '—I deserve everything you throw at me.'

She wanted neither his endearments nor that wonderful, quite marvellous, twitch of his lips. She looked at her watch without the least interest in what time of day it was. 'If I could ask you to finish your explanation,' she suggested pointedly. 'My father will expect his lunch on the table at one o'clock sharp, and Josy likes me to—um—mix the Yorkshire pudding.' Why should Latham Tavenner have the prerogative of lying?

'Your father's part-sponsoring a golf tournament today,' Latham replied with a level look.

She knew that, but she had not expected him to remember. 'So he is, but that doesn't mean that he has to personally attend. He will, of course, later—to present some of the prizes.' Having started to lie, she found herself in too deep not to continue. 'But he always has liked his Sunday lunch at home.'

'He hasn't been to the tournament yet, then?'

'Not yet,' she confirmed. 'So if——' She broke off. Latham was looking at her with a look on his face which she found hard to distinguish. It seemed to fall midway between amusement and—affection!

Affection! scoffed her head, but she was all ears when Latham asked, 'Did I once say you were priceless?' And then, causing her heart to race feverishly, 'You, my dear,' he added, 'are above price.'

Much more of this and she would be forgetting about pride, forgetting that she had to live with herself once he had gone. 'Now what did I do?' she questioned snappily.

'Blatantly lied, for a start,' he replied urbanely.

'You can talk!' she retorted—but couldn't resist asking, 'How did I lie? When did I lie—er—recently?'

'Recently, not five minutes ago.'

'You're suggesting my father is not at home——?'

'I'm not merely suggesting, I'm stating it for a fact,' he cut in unequivocally. And, even as her mouth started to form the word 'how', he was metaphorically pulling the rug from under her feet by adding, 'He was at the golf tournament when I went to see him first thing this morning.'

'You've been to see my father?' she questioned in astonishment, the fact that she had been found out in her 'blatant' lie not seeming to be of importance just then.

'I have,' he agreed.

'But—but...' she spluttered—and got a few more words together to accuse hostilely, 'You didn't think to mention at any time yesterday that you were going to see him this morning!'

'I didn't mention it because I didn't know then,' he replied.

Which left her without argument. She gave what she hoped looked like a careless shrug. 'I confess your way of doing business seems a little haphazard, but——'

'I didn't go to see your father on a business matter,' Latham stated before she could finish.

Her eyes shot wide—he'd gone to see her father on a personal matter! Her foolish heart started to race—and then she remembered, and something inside her froze. 'Josy,' she said, and that was all. But Latham understood.

Why, then, he shook his head she could not tell. Nor could she believe it when, his eyes steady on hers, he told her categorically, 'I was never, at any time, interested in Josy.'

Not for one single solitary moment could she believe it. 'I should thank God your name's not Pinocchio, if I were you—otherwise the length of your nose would hit the other side of this room.'

She stood up, impatient with him that he could tell such lies, and impatient with herself that there was something in her that wanted to believe him, whatever outrageous lie he uttered.

She presented him with her back, loving him even while she hated him—and knew herself for a fool once more when, leaving the couch, he came and stood behind her, placing his hands in a gentle hold on her upper arms. She should have moved away, but she felt helpless to do so. She wanted him to hold her. He had held her oh, so gently last night.

She tried to banish such reminders, and then Latham was speaking again, and was saying, 'My dear, I don't want to hurt you but, in order to clear away all lies and deceits between us, hurt you I'm afraid I must,' and her mouth went dry. His tone, those words 'between us', as if 'us' mattered, made her want to hear every word he had to say. Made her want to stay and listen to what he had to explain—no matter how hurt it sounded as if she might be in the process.

'It—concerns me, then?' she asked chokily, and did not know where to look when Latham turned her round to face him.

'You're trembling,' he murmured.

'It's the weather,' she replied, and nearly died when he brushed a feather-light kiss on her brow.

'Come and sit down,' he urged, and led her not back to the chair she had occupied but to the couch. And it did nothing to quiet her trembling when he sat down on the couch beside her.

'So,' she said as she strove desperately to get herself back together, 'You went to see my father—on a personal matter, you said?'

'That's right,' he agreed, but added very carefully, 'Though, at the beginning, before you and I had met, it was your father who came to see me.'

'Ah!' Belvia exclaimed, and only then realised that, when so much had taken place between her and Latham, she was going to have to remember at all times that her father still wanted him to invest in Fereday Products. 'Hmm—my father came to see you about some business, I expect?' she queried.

But to her astoundment Latham replied, 'No,' going on, 'And if I could spare telling you what I have to, I

would. But I insist you know the truth before...' He
checked, took a deep and steadying breath, and seemed
to change direction when he went on quietly, 'Perhaps,
to save you from tying yourself in knots in trying to
make me think well of your father, I should state that
I now know everything there is to know about him—
including the fact that he's anxious for my company to
invest in his.'

'Oh!' Belvia exclaimed, not certain she did not grow
a little pink about the cheeks.

'Don't be embarrassed,' Latham smiled, watching her,
and nearly sank her yet again when, seeming sensitive
to her every thought, he carefully stated, 'What lies between you and me has nothing to do with money.'

She stared at him for long seconds and knew then that,
whatever it was he had to explain, she wanted to hear
every word. More, as her intelligence started to function
again, she wanted to know, since Latham was again referring to their two selves, what in heaven's name her
father had to do with any of it. She thought it was time
she began to find out.

'You—um—suggested that the first time my father
came to see you—it was not about business.'

'It seemed not—though it's only today that I found
out that that was just a ploy.' Oh, grief! She wanted the
floor to open up and swallow her. Latham too, by the
sound of it, had now learned just how devious her father
could be for his own ends.

'He—er—didn't ask you to invest straight away?'

'Business was never mentioned,' Latham replied and,
making her head all haywire again, he took a gentle hold
of both her hands and held them firmly in his. He seemed
reluctant as he added, 'What your father came to see

me about was the——' his grip tightened '—the affair which he knew you were having with my brother-in-law.'

'The aff——' Witlessly, she stared at him. '*Me!*' she exclaimed, her tone shocked. 'But—but I never——'

'Don't you think I *know* that?' Latham cut in. 'My dear, don't I know, more than anyone, that you've never had an affair in your life?' Warm colour stained her skin again, and suddenly Latham let go of one of her hands and placed an arm about her shoulders. 'Sweet Belvia,' he entreated, 'can you not see how it was with me? How I couldn't rest until I had everything sorted out?'

She was still striving to recover from hearing that her father had gone to him with some tale that she was having an affair with Caroline's husband. But at what Latham had just said her hopes started to rise. 'Is—is that why you—um—rushed off this morning?' Had he gone from her because he thought her—important?

'It was more than time somebody started to be fair to you,' he replied, and Belvia looked at him, loved him, and knew she was never going to be able to concentrate—not while he had his arm about her.

She moved a few inches from him, pulling out of his arm, pulling her hand from his hold. 'Perhaps you'd better start at the very beginning,' she requested, as evenly as she could.

Latham studied every detail of her face. 'It won't be pleasant,' he warned, and she could not help thinking, as he continued to watch her, that should any of what he had to say seem too much for her he would stop immediately—which was enough for her to determine to mask her emotions as much as possible. She wanted, needed, to hear all that there was to hear.

'Caroline told me over the phone,' he began, 'that because of an empathy she immediately felt with you, she found herself telling you of her husband's unfaithfulness to her.'

'I knew beforehand,' Belvia admitted. 'He was at a party I was at this past year. We were introduced and someone told me he was married—but you'd never have known it from the way he was behaving. Caroline's well rid of him.'

'I couldn't agree more. She's had far more to put up with than any woman should.' He paused, and quietly added, 'He's in the middle of some affair right now.'

Belvia stared at him. 'And you thought, because of what my father said, that I was the woman he was having an affair with?'

'I didn't just take your father's word for it,' he replied. 'To tell it as it is, Caroline has been married to Astill for five years, and in those five years for my sister's happiness—since she stated she still wanted him—I've bought off as many women. When some months ago I recognised that look in her eyes that said she was hurting again, I employed a top-class private investigatory firm I'd used before to find out who the current woman was.'

'Good heavens!' Belvia exclaimed, this being a whole new world to her. 'You bought that woman off too?'

But Latham shook his head. 'This time Astill was playing it very cagily, and the investigators, although still on to it, were coming up with nothing.'

'You're sure he was having an affair?'

'That was beyond doubt. Who with, however, was what I needed to know, for my sister's sake.'

'Graeme Astill must have known about the private detectives you'd put on to him before.'

'Caroline, in a weak moment of their last reconciliation, told him of it.'

'I see,' Belvia commented, realising that Graeme Astill, as Latham had said, had been playing this one cagily rather than have his brother-in-law spoil his fun for him. 'But...' She stopped, unable to see any tie-in here with her father. Even while she felt bruised that her father could apparently go to a stranger and say that she was the one Graeme Astill was having an affair with, questions suddenly started queuing up to be answered.

'I don't understand any of this,' she admitted helplessly. 'Why would my father tell you I was having an affair with Caroline's husband when I wasn't? What good...? And how did my father know he was having an affair anyway? And...' Her voice faded as her intelligence really got to work. 'I didn't know my father even knew Graeme Astill!'

'He doesn't,' Latham replied, adding swiftly, 'According to your father, when I insisted this morning on knowing everything there was to know, he'd listened in to an intimate phone conversation his secretary had with Astill some weeks ago.'

Even while Belvia felt slightly sickened—any other person accidentally happening on an intimate conversation would drop the phone like a hot coal, but not her father—she was gasping, 'Vanessa Stanley! Is she the one...?'

'There was not the slightest doubt, your father said, that the two were having an affair. Just as there was no doubt—my name coming up, apparently, and the fact that I was furious to know who the woman was—that they were taking every precaution to prevent me from finding out.'

'Your brother-in-law didn't want you buying Vanessa off?' Belvia queried as she quickly digested that indeed Vanessa Stanley was the one.

'I doubt very much that he mentioned she might be rewarded to give him up, but he no doubt fed her some plausible line about why their affair must remain most secret.'

'But...' She was starting to grow a touch confused, so sought to pin her thoughts on the most basic knowledge. 'So—while my father knew about their affair, neither Vanessa nor your brother-in-law was aware that anyone else knew.'

'They thought they had been much too clever—and but for that phone call, they had,' Latham agreed.

'Yes, but I still don't see——' She broke off. Knowing her devious father well, all at once, with a clarity that was nauseating, she did begin to see. And—while she could hardly credit that her father would use her so— she was quietly stating, 'My father thought that, if he came to you with this piece of information, you'd be so pleased you would look favourably on his request—at some future date naturally——' he could be both devious and wily, her father '—for investment...'

'Had he been speaking the truth, I should, of course, have felt very much indebted to him.'

'But you didn't know he wasn't speaking the truth until...' Oh, grief! It was only last night that he had found out... She flicked a glance at Latham; he looked warmly back at her and reached for her hands. But she took them out of his range. She needed a clear head— even his warm look was devastating, without the feel of his skin against hers. 'So—my father came to you and said that I was the woman your brother-in-law was having an affair with,' she went on, striving desperately hard to keep her head straight.

'Your father's much more subtle than that, Belvia,' Latham replied gently. 'At first he wouldn't tell me anything, but said that he needed to contact my brother-in-law quite urgently—and did I know where he could be found? I suggested he rang him at home, but in the ensuing conversation gathered that he wanted to contact him without my sister knowing.'

'Ah! That was when your protective antennae for your sister went on red alert?'

'Antennae for our sisters we share, you and I,' Latham commented softly, and her heart raced, and her insides fluttered at his tone—and Belvia had to try harder than ever to keep her head straight.

'What happened then?' she asked firmly.

'The upshot was,' Latham answered, seeming now to want it all said and done with quickly, 'what with my refusing to say where he might find my brother-in-law until he told me more, your father had to "reluctantly" confess that Astill was having an affair with his daughter, and that he wanted it stopped.'

Belvia looked away from him, embarrassed that her father could have gone to him with such a tale, embarrassed that Latham should know that her father cared so little for her.

She swallowed hard when she felt Latham take her hands in his warm clasp, and she had never loved him more when he said, as though seeing her embarrassment, as if trying to ease it and her hurt, 'His business is in sorry trouble, my darling.'

Oh, Latham, she thought in panic, her embarrassment and pain swiftly sent on their way by that utterly unbelievable 'my darling'. Perhaps he always calls every woman he has made love to 'my darling', she made herself think—anything rather than believe, because she loved him so, what her heart wanted to believe—that his 'my darling' meant that he had a little caring for her.

'Having learned who "the woman" was, having believed my father, you told him to leave it with you—that you would stop it for him?' Belvia questioned, as coolly as she was able.

'I saw no reason to disbelieve him,' Latham owned. 'Though naturally I went and saw Astill and confronted him with the fact that I knew your name.'

'He didn't deny it?' she questioned, startled.

'He looked astonished when I trotted out your name— as well he might,' Latham replied. 'Only I thought his astonishment stemmed from the fact that I'd found out what he was trying to keep a closely guarded secret. But he recovered fast and, as quick-thinking and as devious as your father, must have realised that if I thought you were the one it would give him more freedom with the Stanley woman. And I was left in the frustrating position of being unable to lay a fist on him—because Caroline still wanted him and because of the promise I'd made to her—and, because your father had said you had money of your own, of being unable to attempt to buy you off.'

'Why didn't you come and ask me about it?' she asked, entirely unthinkingly, then halted in her tracks. 'You would never have believed any denial I made, anyway, would you?'

'For my sins—I confess, no. Though not without cause,' he added.

'What cause...?' she began, then remembered. 'I confirmed it for you myself, didn't I?—that night we met, that night when you came to dinner and...'

'And you went out, tossing into the room those immortal words, "After dinner is the only time he can get away from his wife".'

'No wonder you looked furious!'

'Furious, and more determined than ever to put a stop to it. By that time I'd reasoned that either you were as brazen as hell, or that Astill, rather than have you warned off, had kept it to himself that I knew you were his mistress. I realised too that, as we'd agreed, your father had said nothing to you about the fact that I knew.'

'Why would he say anything?' Belvia put in, not liking her father very much just then.

'Try not to be upset,' Latham pressed. 'The whole thing's a mess, a nightmare. But once we've got it all unravelled...' That warm look was in his eyes again—and suddenly Belvia found herself in a state of not knowing what to believe in any more, and looked quickly away.

'Why did you accept my father's invitation to dinner that night?' she asked, again hoping that if she went back to the beginning it might be of some help.

'Your father had stressed that, while your sister would do anything he asked of her, you were as intractable as the devil. But, to my mind, while you plainly did not hold the sanctity of marriage in the same high regard that he did, I felt that, intractable or no, you must have a weak spot somewhere. I needed to see you, preferably over a meal, where you'd be forced to spend more than a few minutes in my company.'

'Did you find it—my weak spot?'

'Astonishingly quickly. No sooner had I seen the way you were hovering protectively over your sister while your father introduced Josy and me than I knew that there were no lengths you wouldn't go to for her. That protection of Josy was further endorsed, should I have needed it endorsing, when each time I tried to engage her in conversation you answered for her.'

Belvia realised that, since he was so protective of his own sister, that same trait in her must have been easily recognisable. She let go a long-drawn breath as she suddenly recalled how he had categorically stated that he had never at any time been interested in Josy. 'You decided to try to get through to intractable me by using my sister?' she asked.

'I'd never seen anything so clear-cut, so evident,' he replied. 'I saw at once that I had only to make the smallest play for your shy sister—and you would be in there protecting her like a shot.'

'You thought to ask me to give up your brother-in-law in exchange for not pursuing Josy?'

'That was perhaps the obvious thing to do. But, discussing that solution with your father—and we've been in frequent touch throughout,' he inserted, 'he—who knew you better than me, remember—felt you would verbally agree to give up Astill but would continue with your clandestine meetings and tell Astill, who would only become more cagey than ever. Which left me deciding that, to limit your time with your lover, I would, for a start, take you on myself.'

'You were so certain I would go out with you? That Josy would go out with you?'

'Josy, so your father said—and, remember, I'd no idea of what little game he was playing in the background— would agree if he mentioned that it would please him if she would do so. But you, love, as I recall, I didn't have to invite out at all those first couple of times—you just turned up.'

'But—you weren't expecting me, that first time. That time I arrived in the car you sent you were expecting Josy.'

'I was expecting none other than you, believe me,' Latham corrected her quietly. 'I knew before I rang Josy on Monday that your father had that morning spoken with her on the subject of her being more friendly to his guests in future. Just as I knew that she would come looking for you the moment after she'd agreed to come out with me that evening.'

'You probably also knew that I'd try to phone you to say she couldn't come,' Belvia suggested, and he smiled, and her heart fluttered crazily.

'Your father rang to tip me off about ten seconds before you rang,' he owned. 'Just enough time for me to instruct my PA that I was out of town should any Miss Belvia Fereday ring.'

'But—you say you were expecting none other than me,' Belvia reminded him and, as she remembered, 'You looked amazed to see me—as if you couldn't believe...!'

'If I stared at you when you got out of that car, my dear, it was not from amazement,' he interrupted, 'but because I was stunned.'

'Stunned?'

Latham nodded. 'Quite simply, I thought you the most lovely creature I'd ever seen.'

'You d-did?' she croaked.

'Oh, yes,' he breathed. 'And that was when everything started to go wrong.'

'Wrong?'

He smiled. 'Wrong, right—I soon didn't know where the hell I was,' he revealed. 'All I knew for sure was that if by any small chance Josy had turned up that evening, then I'd have taken every care of her.'

Her heart warmed some more to him that, having seen how dreadfully shy her sister was, he would have afforded her some of the same regard he gave his own sister. 'But it wasn't Josy who turned up—but me.'

'Indeed it was you,' he agreed. 'And I looked at you, sat beside you in the theatre, and life was never the same again. I had to leave you in the interval to go and try to get my head back together.'

Belvia shot him a startled look. 'Y-You're saying I—um—affected you in some...? That you were aware of me during the——'

'I'm saying all of that,' Latham continued. 'I'm saying that while I wanted you there, where photographers were, where there was every chance Astill would see a picture of you with me, I at the same time felt the stirrings of jealousy when I returned to find Rodney Phillips sitting in my seat—taking up my space with you.'

'Oh, heavens,' she whispered shakily, any intelligence she might have been blessed with suddenly deserting her—what did he mean?

'"Oh, heavens," it was, little one,' Latham stated gently. 'There was I, when I'd had no such intention, taking you on to dinner—and there you were—an entirely new experience for me—walking out on me when dinner had barely got started.'

'I—um—told your chauffeur that you wouldn't need him again that night,' she confessed, her brain-power still scattered.

'I know—he told me the next morning. I knew I was in trouble when I found myself laughing at your sauce.'

'You were—in trouble?'

'What would you call it when the next time I saw you— you again turning up in your sister's place—chemistry should rear its head and I should start to desire you?'

Some of her intelligence stirred—from what she could remember, that desire had not been one-sided. 'I've— never felt like that before,' she owned shakily.

'Now, I know it—then, I didn't. Are you going to forgive me?' he asked.

She felt on shaky ground again. 'Should I?'

'Oh, sweet love,' he groaned and, as if he could not take much more of her sitting even that little bit away, he put his arm about her, and she did not pull away, but went willingly. Latham held her quietly to him for several seconds, before going on to tell her, 'Your father had worked it all out very carefully. He did not rush into it but—he told me this morning—spent several days going over his plan to put me in his debt—to owe him a favour. He believed he had all the angles covered. He'd asked me not to mention to you that I knew you were having an affair with my brother-in-law—because he knew you would deny it. He had also calculated that I might go and see Astill and give him the name of his lady-love, but, by the very nature of Astill wanting to keep his real lady-love's name a secret, he reckoned—as in fact did happen—that Astill would let me go on believing his mistress was you—or anyone else, for that matter. Provided I didn't come up with the name Vanessa Stanley he'd got nothing to worry about.'

'Did Caroline think I was——?'

'No,' Latham answered before she could finish. 'She knew he was having an affair, of course, but she still doesn't know who with. And now, thank the Lord, she no longer cares. But, on the subject of caring, your father thought he had it all meticulously worked out before he came to see me.' He paused, and then, his eyes watchful on her, he went on carefully, 'What he had not taken into account, though, was that having met you I should start to care—about you.'

Her eyes went huge in her face, and her throat dried again. 'C-Care...?' It was as much as she could manage.

Latham looked tenderly down at her and smiled. 'Oh, yes, sweet love, care,' he breathed. 'From your father's viewpoint, once he'd got the investment he needed signed and sealed by my company, you need never have been any the wiser. He'd planned to tell me you had dropped Astill—and he could hardly be blamed if Astill subsequently took up with his secretary.' Devious, Belvia realised, was hardly a strong enough word for her father. 'In his opinion, whether I thought Astill would have told you of my knowing you were the one was immaterial. And you, in your ignorance of what was going on, were hardly likely to mention his name either. So far as your father was concerned, I could think you as brazen about it as I liked. But, while everything began the way he calculated it might, what he did not know was that I soon started to love your spirit, to care about your vulnerability.' She stared at him transfixed, and was barely breathing when, cupping the side of her face with one hand, he breathed oh, so tenderly, 'In fact, my darling, he had not calculated that I should start to fall in love with you.'

'You—love me?' she choked huskily.

'So very much,' he replied softly, and placed the tenderest of kisses on her slightly parted lips. 'I've known it, even as I've tried to deny it, from that night you came to my apartment to explain about Josy—only never got round to it. I followed you to the kitchen and I wanted you as you wanted me, but you said you were confused. And it was then that, as I recognised your vulnerability, as I held you, I knew confusion too. Because it wasn't just desire I felt for you—and it wasn't supposed to be like that. You were a hard case, you weren't supposed to be vulnerable—yet you were. But as we started to make love it was wonderful, different—head-swimmingly different—not like the time before, when I'd jeered at you for sleeping around and you nearly fractured my cheekbone for my trouble. This time you were putting a stop to our lovemaking, and daring to tell me that it wasn't right.'

'I'm sorry.'

'*You're* apologising?'

'I wanted to... That night I wanted...' Her voice started to fracture. 'Only, that first time, my—er—first time, I wanted it to be with someone who loved me.'

Latham pulled back and looked deeply into her beautiful eyes. 'Are you saying what I think you're saying, my shy darling?' he asked gently, yet with a hint of strain there in his voice too. 'Are you saying what every instinct, what everything I've learned—not been told—about you is saying? That—that night—you were in love—with me?'

'I—couldn't believe it. But it was true,' she replied on a low whisper.

'That you love me?' It seemed, with all the evidence there, that he still needed to hear it.

She smiled and, when an hour ago wild horses would not have dragged that truthful confession from her, 'I do love you,' she shyly agreed.

'Sweet love,' he groaned, and gathered her close up to him, saying not another word for long, long minutes. Not even kissing her but, as though he had been through great, great torment and had a need to hold her—hold her knowing that she loved no one but him—just holding her close up against his heart.

Then, gently, he kissed her and pulled back, as if hoping to see the confirmation of her words in her eyes. And it was there.

'Oh, I adore you!' he breathed, and kissed her and held her and kissed her some more—before pulling back, and, as if striving hard to get his head together, saying, 'This can't be, I've been so foul to you—I don't deserve that you should love me.'

'True,' she laughed, for just then she was so full of emotion it was that or tears.

'Oh, I love you, I love you, I love you,' he stated throatily, and kissed her and went on, as if searching for words of comfort for any hurt she felt, 'In your father's favour, he told me that had he known I intended taking you away for the weekend he would have found some way of preventing you from going.'

'Most likely because he felt his plan was at risk—I expect you'd have said that your brother-in-law would be there too.' Suddenly she could not weigh that up at all, and just had to say, 'I don't understand why Graeme

Astill accepted your invitation if he knew that I'd be th...' Her voice faded, realisation coming to her. 'You didn't tell him I'd be there, did you?'

'What a mess has been created!' Latham replied. 'But, since I want you to know absolutely everything, I have to confess that, apart from alerting Caroline to keep the weekend free and to make sure her husband was available, I'd not issued any invitation to Rose Cottage when I came to see you on Friday.'

'You hadn't? But...' She stared at him. 'But you said...'

'Lies, all round, have been flying about like confetti,' Latham confirmed. 'I lied to you when I said on Friday morning that I'd invited people down to Wiltshire. But, in my defence, sweet love, I'd come to see you on Wednesday purely because I felt such a need to see you, to hear you.'

'I'd asked if I could ring you...'

'Exactly—but you hadn't, and thoughts of you were driving me insane. I decided to come and see you and play it by ear. You then told me of the dreadful time Josy was going through and how she was a rare and precious person—and all I could think was that you were a rare and precious person too, and how your pain was my pain, but how I was going to have to hurt you and soon—because I just couldn't take much more.'

'Oh, my love!' Belvia exclaimed, the endearment slipping out purely because she could not stop it.

'Oh, that was worth waiting to hear,' he murmured, and gently kissed her—but then manfully resumed. 'So, there was I, falling deeper and deeper in love with you and wanting only to protect you, while at the same time determined to break this affair you were having, and soon. By Friday, after two nights of torment, I knew I couldn't take any more.'

'So you came here and told me a pack of lies,' she teased lovingly.

'Oh, God—you're marvellous,' he groaned, kissed her, and scraped together some more determination to continue. 'With everything erupting in my head, all I could do was concentrate on the facts as I knew them and—in danger of losing my grip on logic too—try to think logically. I knew Astill and his mistress had discussed me, and could only calculate that, if anything, you'd have told him I was after your sister.'

'Because it was Josy you had invited to the theatre and to dinner at your flat?'

Latham nodded. 'It also seemed safe to assume that—forgive me, love—because of the way you responded to me when I held you in my arms, you were unlikely to have told him about that.'

'A fair assumption,' she mumbled, going a little pink about the cheeks.

'You're adorable!' Latham exclaimed, and had to kiss her once more.

'And...' she prompted.

He gave her a loving look, but went on, 'Which in turn gave me the idea for this weekend.'

'You thought to put us all together?'

'While part of me was all against the thought of having him and you together at Rose Cottage—I needed it all settled. I've no time whatsoever for Astill but, from what I knew of him, I just couldn't see him taking his mistress sleeping with another man under the same roof—and not ending the affair. The result would be, I thought, that my sister would have what she wanted and, more importantly to me now, you too would be free. All I had to do was to ensure Astill didn't hear a whisper of it from you, before I'd got you incommunicado.'

'Incommunicado?' she queried—and then light dawned. 'You followed me up to my room, ostensibly to carry my case down, but really...'

'To make sure you didn't phone him,' Latham finished for her.

'You read my note to Josy too, in——'

'In case it was a note to your lover—and never loved you more when I realised that for Josy to believe what you'd written about going to stay with your retired friend who was feeling low, it must be the kind of typical thing you would do. Just as it was typical of you that you'd arrange for someone to exercise her horse while you were away.'

'Actually, Josy very bravely managed to exercise Hetty herself,' Belvia replied, and, her happiness brimming over, 'Oh, I do love you, Mr Tavenner.'

'Kiss me when you say that, woman,' he growled, and she did, and it was quite some minutes later that they breathlessly broke apart. Looking down into her slightly flushed face, he said, 'That, I think, was what helped me to keep going.'

'A kiss?' She was too bemused to think straight and, his eyes caressing her, he gave her an adoring smile.

'How could you be in love with him, or anyone else, yet respond so ardently to me? I was in love with you and didn't want to look at another woman, much less return an embrace.'

'Oh, tell me more!' she cried.

'Minx,' he laughed, and she loved him.

'So—um...' She tried to get her head back together. 'So what made you think I'd go away with you in the first place?' She managed to get a question together.

'Was there any doubt, sweetheart?' he asked gently.

She remembered his threat to Josy. 'No, I suppose not,' she smiled.

'And you don't hate me?'

'How could I?'

'How could you not? Though, if it's any consolation, I nearly blew it when you looked up at me, all big brown eyes, and asked for my promise not to come over all amorous. That was when I wanted to hold you safe in my arms, to protect you, and to tell you everything was all right.'

'But everything was not all right, was it?'

'Very far from being all right,' he agreed. 'So off we went, and I so enjoyed being with you, just the two of us—lunch—the supermarket—it was all wonderful; you were wonderful. We reached Rose Cottage and I began to hate like hell that I was going to have to get on the phone to my sister and invite her and her husband down.'

'Oh, darling,' she sighed—but then cried, suddenly remembering, 'You phoned Caroline from your car-phone!'

'I did,' he confirmed. 'I had to. I had to kill whatever it was between you and Astill dead.'

'You were beginning to doubt I was having an affair with him?' she questioned, thinking that was what he meant. But he shook his head.

'The evidence was too strong. And yet you seemed oddly nervous when I came into the bedroom while you were bed-making. Something wasn't right—I knew it.'

'You held me in your arms,' she recalled.

'And that *did* seem right,' he smiled. 'It felt as though that was where you belonged—it felt right for me, so it had to be right for you too, didn't it?'

'Oh, it was,' she beamed.

'Oh, love,' he murmured, and held her close. 'I must have been blind. Everything was adding up to you being a totally different woman from the one I'd been led to believe you were—yet still I was ready to believe the worst.'

'You were determined to believe I was having an affair with your brother-in-law?'

'I did ask you on Friday night if you had a problem with it when you admitted that you knew him.'

'I only met him the one time—at that party. But that was long enough to realise he has a loose mouth, and would see no need to keep from any mutual acquaintances, friends, that I'd been rooming with you...'

'Oh, dear love—that was what you meant. I thought...'

'I see now what you thought,' she laughed. 'You thought I was saying I had a problem because if I was rooming with anyone, it should be him.'

'You've so much to forgive me for. I only began to realise just how much when last night I held you sleeping in my arms.'

'Oh, Latham,' she cried. 'I tried so hard to be asleep before you came up the stairs.' She smiled as she told him, 'Brute that you are, I was wide awake—and you came up and went out like a light.'

'No way!'

Startled, she stared at him. 'You didn't? But—your breathing was...'

'The same as yours.' His smile matched hers. 'We were both pretending like hell. For my part I was in torment, wanting to come to you, while at the same time knowing that I wanted more from you than just one night.'

'Oh, darling,' she sighed, all her fears about how little he must think of her gone forever.

'Sweet love, I wanted your affair with Astill over, ended, out of the way, before I claimed you. Then your breathing really did relax and I knew you *were* asleep. But just as I'd started to grow calmer, so you suddenly started yelling. I was out of bed, had to wake you. Yet while I was desperately trying to be strong you suddenly leaned against me and—I was lost.'

'Blaming me again?' she teased lightly.

'Never again,' he murmured, and laid his lips on her hair, and after a minute or so of just holding her quietly he told her how it had been with him. 'At first I just couldn't get over this stupendous loving we had shared, couldn't get over the wonderful and astonishing discovery I'd made about you. I couldn't believe it, and but for the fact that you were sleeping naked in my arms, I might well have believed I was dreaming after all. And then, as daylight started to enter our room, I began to grow angry.'

'Angry? With me?' she asked, looking at him wide-eyed.

'Not with you—never again with you, sweet love. Though at first I was tempted to wake you so you might answer some of the questions that were spinning furiously through my mind.'

'Why didn't you—wake me, I mean?'

Latham smiled tenderly down at her. 'The reason, lovely Belvia, being that as I looked at you my heart was so filled with love for you that I wanted to shower you with kisses. And yet, should I have kissed you gently awake, then I could not be certain that I wouldn't be lost again, that I wouldn't make love to you again.'

'You didn't want to?' she asked, unaware of her naïveté.

'Sweet innocent,' Latham crooned, 'I have so much to teach you. But not then. Then I owed you more than that I should again make you mine. First I wanted answers—not from you, I realised. You, my darling, owed me nothing. But somebody did.'

'My father?'

'He'd come to me, seemingly worried to death that you were having an affair with my brother-in-law. You'd confirmed you had a married man-friend. My brother-in-law himself, when challenged, admitted he was the one—a smoke-screen to stop me finding out who he was really seeing, I now realise. As I also realised, as you lay sleeping, that your unfortunate remark stemmed purely from the fact that you were too spirited to be put down by my clear dislike of what I thought you to be.' He kissed the tip of her nose lest that comment in any way bruised her.

'To be honest, I was feeling most awkward at the start of the evening that my father was entertaining you purely for his own ends. Though, as the evening went on,' she felt she should confess, 'I couldn't help thinking that perhaps you and my father deserved each other.'

Latham smiled, as if in agreement. But his smile had gone when he revealed, 'I thought back to that time when this morning I set about looking for answers. I've met all types through my business but didn't know what to believe about Edwin Fereday. I wanted to declare my

love—dared to hope that the hint of jealousy I'd hoped
I'd heard in your voice when you'd asked about the lady-
friends I'd brought down to Rose Cottage might mean
you cared just a little. I'd had to dismiss it at the time,
but resurrected it again when I realised Astill was nothing
to you. I added that hope to the wonderful way you had
given yourself to me—and, hardly daring to breathe for
fear of waking you, I took my clothes out to the landing
and got dressed.'

'You got dressed out...'

'I didn't want to disturb you. From the very beginning you had not been treated right. You owed neither
me nor anyone else a thing—but I was owed! From the
beginning I'd been misled. It was time I collected a few
answers.'

'You went to see my father?'

'By a stroke of luck Astill was wandering about
downstairs, looking for aspirins.'

'You asked him first...'

'It didn't get as far as that. Before I could grab him
by the throat and tell him to start talking he had the
temerity to ask—the implication obvious—if I'd had a
good night. Sorry, my darling, but there are types like
him around.'

'Obviously you didn't reply.'

'He was measuring his length on the floor before I
could speak—it was truly one of the most satisfying ex-
periences of my life. But, before I could stand him up
and repeat the pleasure, Caroline was standing there,
witness to how I was too enraged to remember my
promise never to hit him. I couldn't regret what I'd done,
but was glad to hear her say thanks, and add as she
stepped over him and came out to my car with me that

she intended to divorce him. Which, my darling, left me with just one more person to see before I came back to claim you.'

Oh, how wonderful that sounded. And oh, how she wished that she had dumped her pride and waited at Rose Cottage. 'Oh, if only I'd known you intended to come back.'

'You'd have saved me going half demented, hope fading with every mile, when I left Rose Cottage for a second time today—this time in search of you.'

'Oh, Latham!' she cried, and leaned forward and kissed him. Then she pulled back and, her brain-patterns all haywire, from somewhere found enough intelligence to suggest, 'The—um—first time you left was to go in search of my father?'

'And did he have a tale to tell!'

'A believable one?'

'At first, no. Only when I told him I knew absolutely everything, and he slipped up to the small extent that he revealed he was considering—only considering, mind—approaching my company for some capital, did I get an inkling of what he was really about. How, incredibly, he was prepared to use both you and your sister, and anybody else he had to, to keep Fereday Products in business. He wriggled like hell, but at last I got the whole of it out of him.'

'H-How did you leave things?' Belvia asked, aware that she loved her parent but not feeling she owed him anything.

'I said something to the effect that I'd be in touch, and raced off to Wiltshire.'

Gently their lips met, and for a while Belvia was oblivious to everything save that she loved Latham and that he, unbelievably, loved her. Then, his look tender, Latham was pulling back.

'You're heady stuff, Miss Fereday,' he stated, his voice thick in his throat. 'I'm trying like hell to remember that it's Sunday morning, I'm in the sitting-room in your home, and that your sister could come in at any moment.'

'I don't think she will,' Belvia smiled, knowing it for a fact. But then, trying to get her head together after the nonsense he had made of it, she asked, 'Um—er—will you be in touch with my father about his business, do you suppose? Er—will you invest in his company, do you——?' She broke off. Latham was looking at her with a most serious look in his eyes. 'What...?' she questioned chokily, and felt one of his hands come up again to the side of her face.

'What do you think, my sweet love? Should I let him have the investment he needs—send in my own men to ride shotgun? He won't like it—but he won't get a better offer. Or——' his arm about her shoulders tightened '—should I let my father-in-law's firm go under?'

'Father-in-law?' she croaked.

'In case you haven't realised it, dearest love, that's what he'll be to me when, as soon as I can arrange it, you become my wife.'

'Oh!' she gasped, pink tingeing her cheeks, her heart racing fit to burst—and Latham started to look anxious.

'You *are* going to marry me, aren't you?' he demanded sharply. 'Hell's teeth! God knows I don't deserve you, but——'

'I'd like very much to marry you,' Belvia cut in quickly, her voice little above a whisper.

He checked. 'What did you say?' he asked urgently.

'I'd like to be Mrs Latham Tavenner as soon as you can arrange it, please,' she said, and heard his small sound of utter delight—and the next she knew she was crushed up against his heart—where she wanted to be.

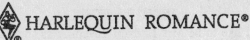

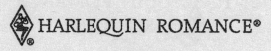

HARLEQUIN ROMANCE®

brings you

Romances that take the family to heart!

What could be better for Christmas than a warm and wonderful Yuletide romance with a man, a woman and an adorable little girl? Betty Neels's latest novel, A CHRISTMAS WISH (#3389), has all these things. Which is why it's our Family Ties book for December.

For Olivia Harding the offer of employment at an exclusive private school had come as something of a godsend. With little experience she hadn't expected to find a job so easily, let alone one that still brought her into contact with her former boss, the eminent Dutch surgeon Haso van der Eisler. Of course, his frequent visits to the school had more to do with his goddaughter Nel than her own limited attractions.

Nel was a lonely, fatherless girl, and that Haso should marry the child's glamorous mother seemed obvious to Olivia, but that didn't stop her wishing.... Would she find Haso or heartbreak under the mistletoe this Christmas?

"Betty Neels works her magic to bring us a touching love story."
—*Romantic Times*